MEL BAY PRESENTS

UKULELE

CHORD SOLOS • IN C TUNING

BY NEIL GRIFFIN

D1458083

CD contents

1	Tuning [1:01]	12	Hail, Hail the Gangs All Here [:49]
2	Aloha Oe [1:21]	13	The World is Waiting for the Sunrise [1:30]
3	Ja-Da [:59]	14	Bill Bailey [1:39]
4	Chinatown, My Chinatown [1:32]	15	For Me and My Gal [2:27]
5	When the Saints Go Marching In [:46]	16	Margie [1:48]
6	Song of the Islands [1:13]	17	I Want a Girl [1:46]
7	You Tell Me Your Dream, I'll Tell You Mine [1:51]	18	In the Good Old Summertime [1:51]
8	Just Because [1:28]	19	The Sheik of Araby [1:36]
9	Melody of Love [1:57]	20	By the Light of the Silvery Moon [1:22]
10	Sweetheart of Sigma Chi [1:06]	21	Whispering [1:52]
11	Smiles [2:14]	22	Oh, You Beautiful Doll [1:25]

Thanks to Rob Carlisle, Berklee graduate and friend of my son, for playing the uke solos on the CD.

MEL BAY

1 2 3 4 5 6 7 8 9 0

Visit us on the Web at www.melbay.com — E-mail us at email@melbay.com

CONTENTS

PARTS OF THE UKE

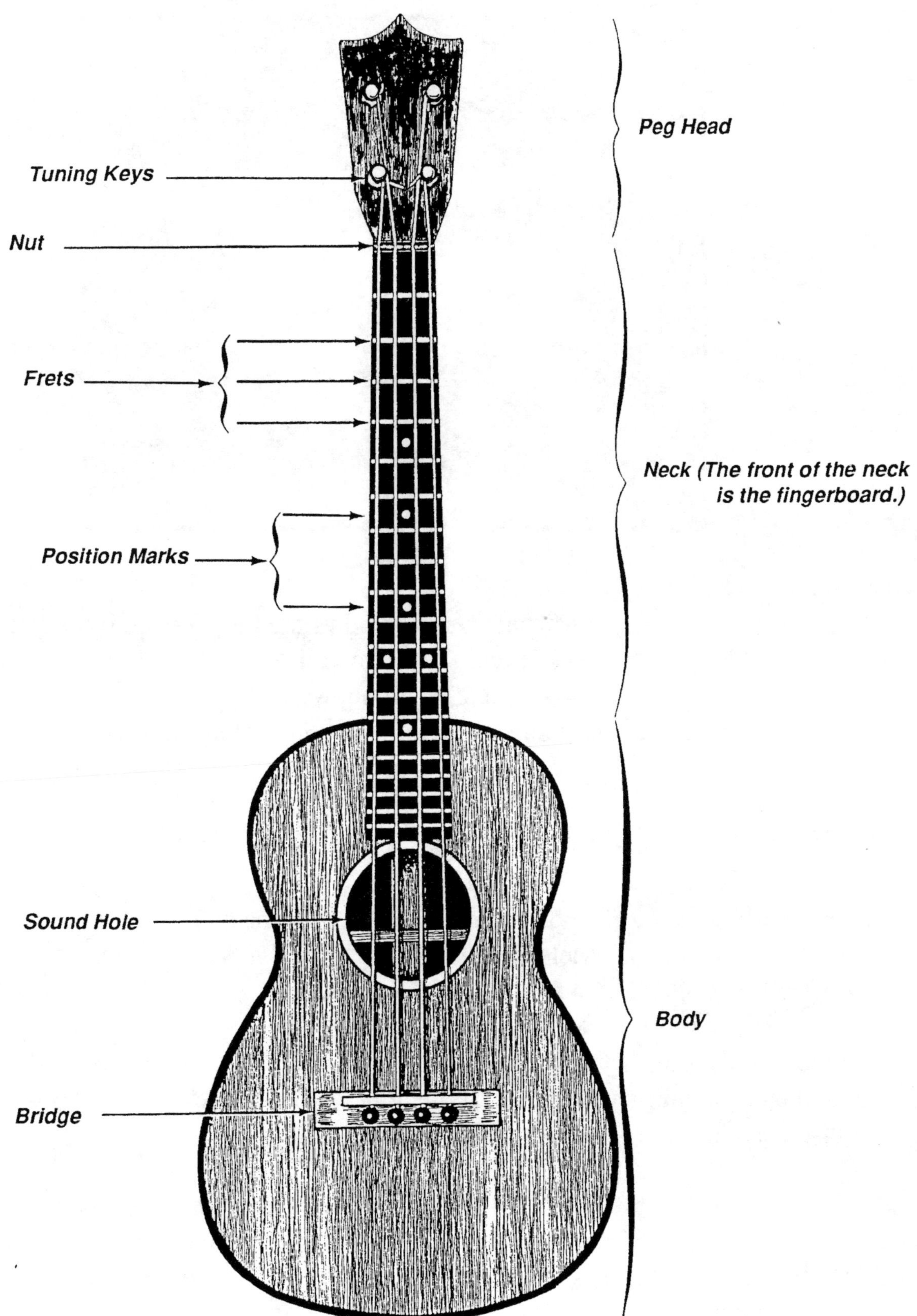

Peg Head
Tuning Keys
Nut
Frets
Neck (The front of the neck is the fingerboard.)
Position Marks
Sound Hole
Body
Bridge

HOLDING THE UKE

The author's grandson, Michael Griffin, shows the proper way to hold the uke.
Hold the uke above your waist
Hold it at a slightly upward angle
Use your right forearm to hold the uke against your body

Other information about this book

If you do not have some basic knowledge of the uke then the author strongly suggests that in addition to this book, you use Mel Bay's *You Can Teach Yourself Uke* (MB94809) to learn the basics of strumming.

Although there is usually only one chord diagram for each note in the solos. When a note is longer than the one count, most players fill the time with extra strokes on the longer notes. The compact disc contains some examples of this.

In addition to the normal down (/) and up (V) strokes the author often uses the "brush stroke" as follows: curl the fingers on your right hand and starting with the 4th finger followed by the 3rd, the 2nd, and the 1st - brush across the strings in a downward direction with the back of each fingernail. This is very effective for long notes.

WAYS TO TUNE YOUR UKE

1. Tune it to a Piano

This method will use "*C tuning*." In C tuning the strings are tuned to the following notes:

First String ....A①
Second String ....E②
Third String ....C③
Fourth String ....G④

On a piano the notes are found as follows:

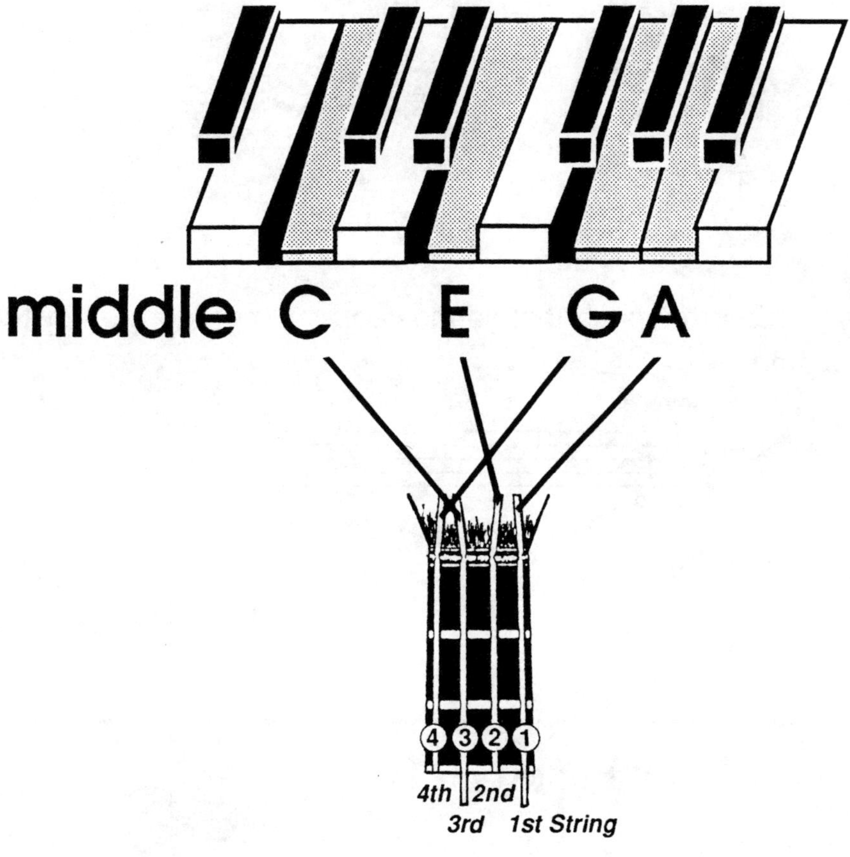
middle C E G A
④③②①
4th 2nd
3rd 1st String

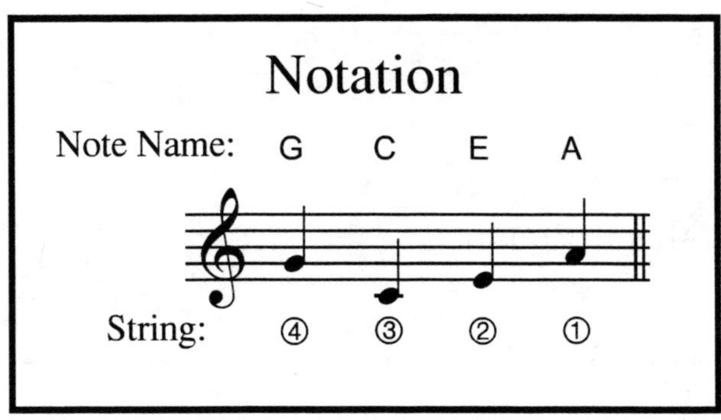
Notation
Note Name: G C E A
String: ④ ③ ② ①

2. Tune with a Pitch Pipe

Ukulele pitch pipes can be purchased from most music stores. Blow into the appropriate sound hole and tune the string to the correct pitch.

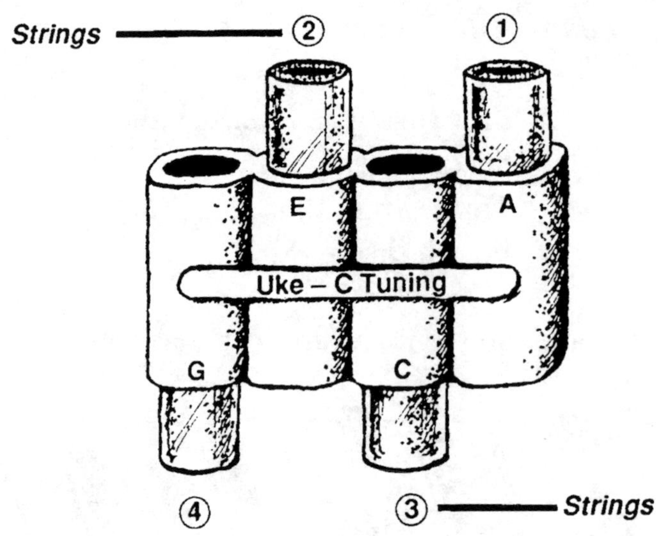
Strings
②
①
E
A
Uke – C Tuning
G
C
④
③
Strings

3. Tuning By Ear

Once you tune your first string to a pitch that sounds correct (not too high or too low), you can use the following expression:

My dog has fleas.
Note Name: G C E A
String: ④ ③ ② ①

Important Hint

There is usually a tiny screw in the back of each tuning peg. Be sure each screw is tight. If they are loose, the strings will slip, and you will not be able to tune the uke. (Do not tighten them, however, so tight that the tuning peg will not turn!)

Peg-Tightening Screw

THE LEFT HAND

The following illustrations show the proper positioning of the left hand. Notice that only the *tips* of the left-hand fingers are used to press down the strings. (Be sure your fingers do not accidentally touch the adjacent string. If this happens, the adjacent string will sound muffled or deadened.) Be sure the thumb is on the back of the neck, *not* wrapped around the side. Finally, when you press down a string, place your finger behind the metal fret, *not* on top of it.

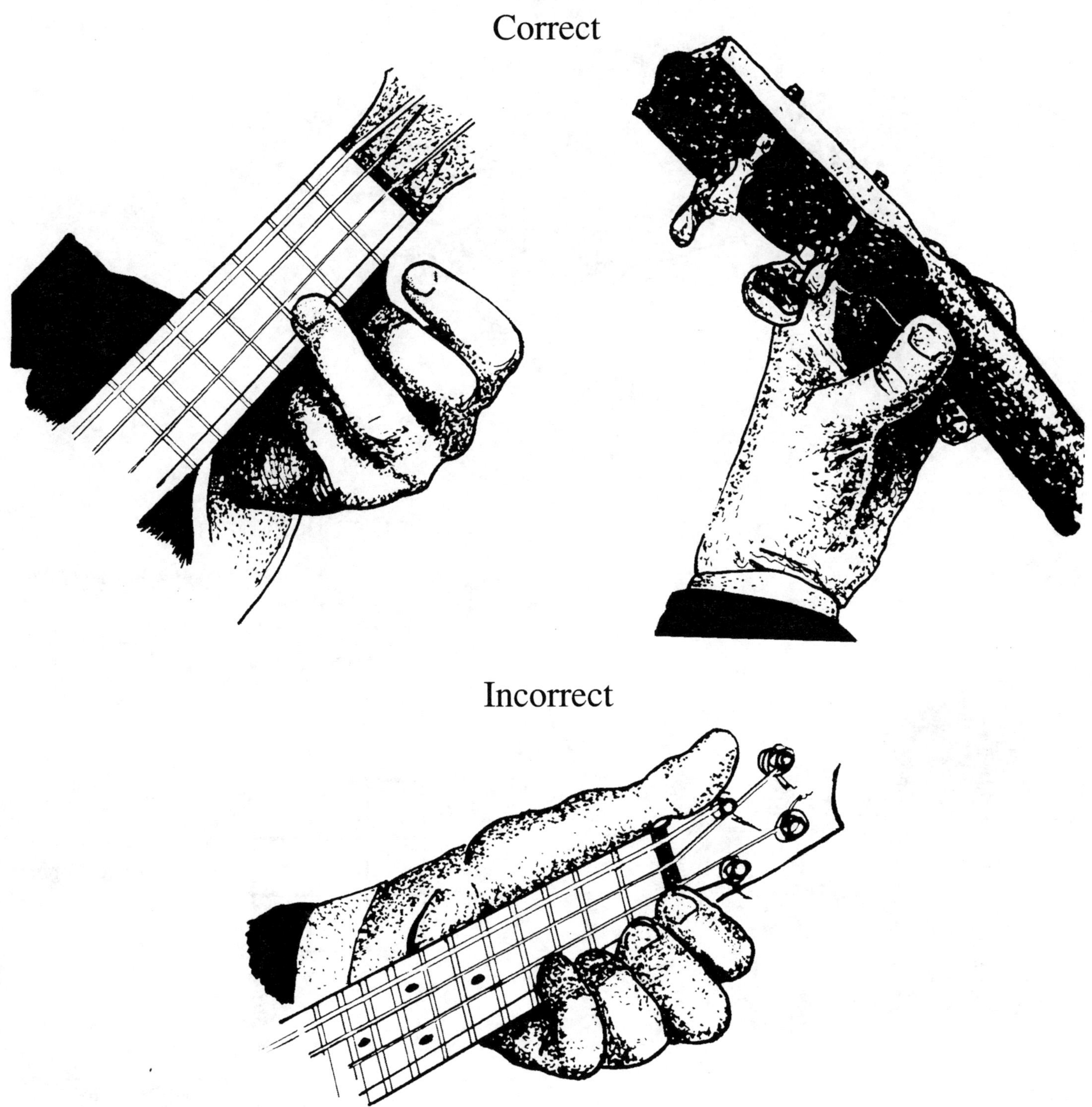
Correct
Incorrect

HOW TO READ CHORD DIAGRAMS

A chord diagram shows you where to place your fingers in order to play a chord. The vertical lines are the strings. The horizontal lines are the frets. The circled numbers are left-hand fingers.

Left-hand fingers are numbered as follows:

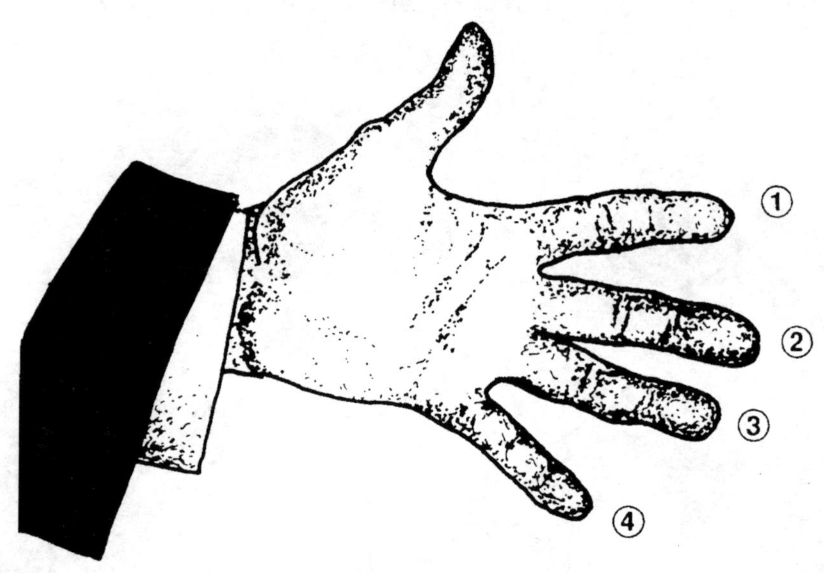

①
②
③
④

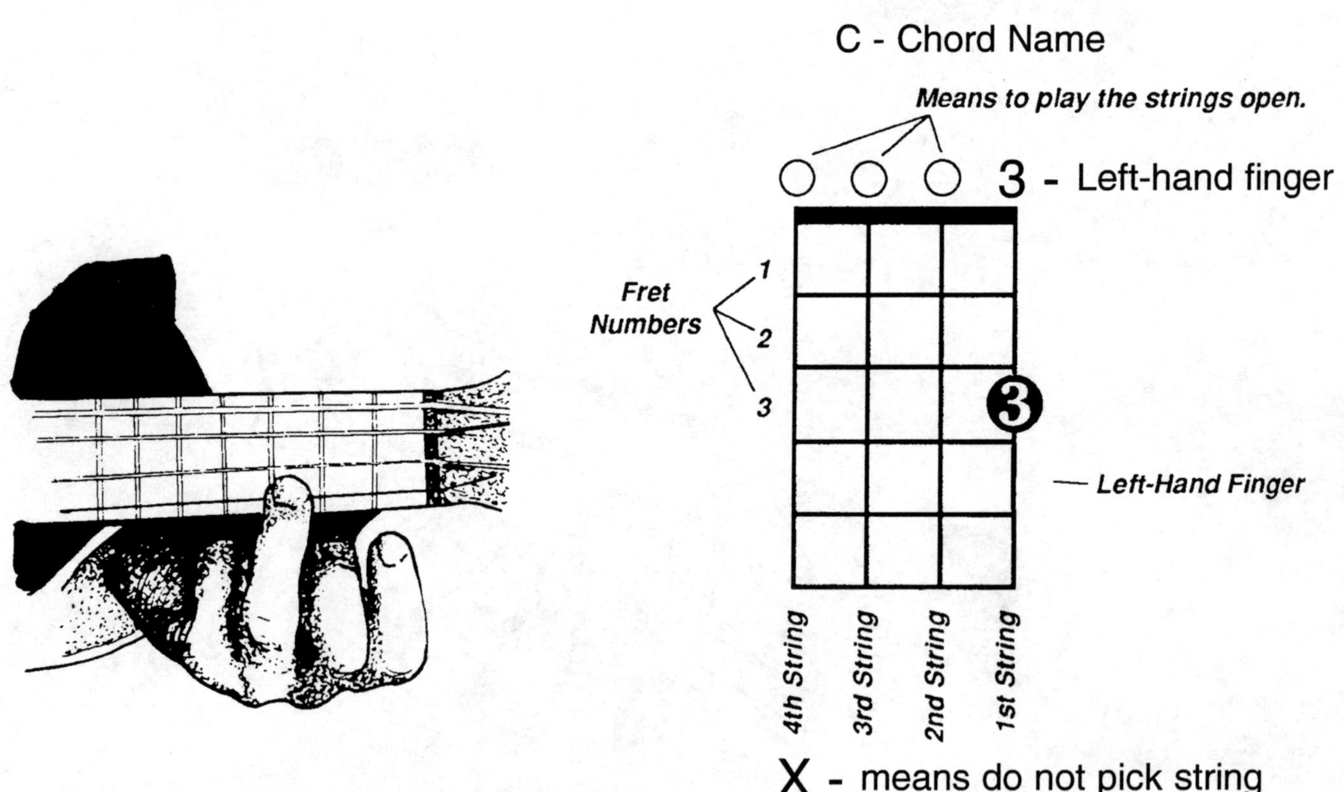

C - Chord Name
Means to play the strings open.
3 - Left-hand finger
Fret Numbers
1
2
3
3
— Left-Hand Finger
4th String
3rd String
2nd String
1st String
X - means do not pick string

ALOHA OE

(Farewell to Thee)

COMPACT
disc
DIGITAL AUDIO
2

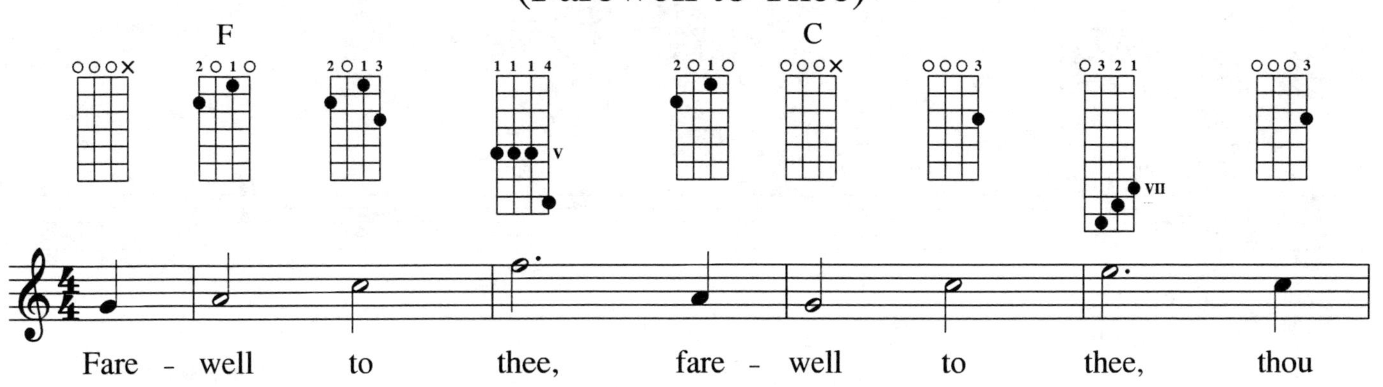

F
C
Fare - well to thee, fare - well to thee, thou

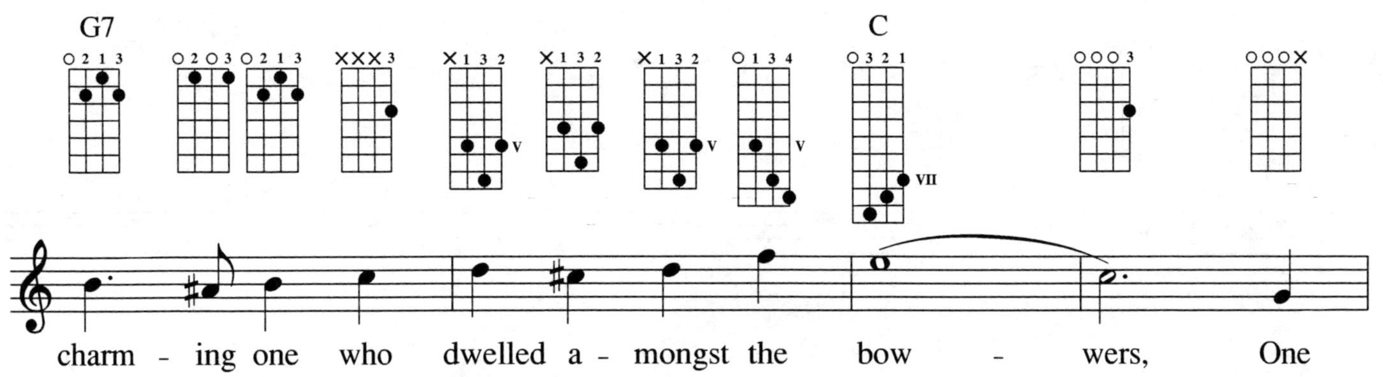

G7
C
charm - ing one who dwelled a - mongst the bow - wers, One

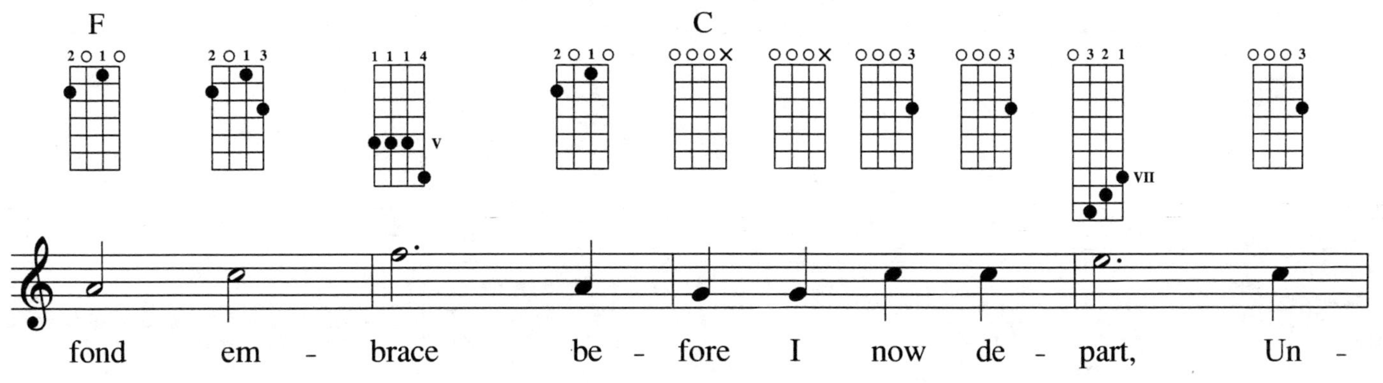

F
C
fond em - brace be - fore I now de - part, Un -

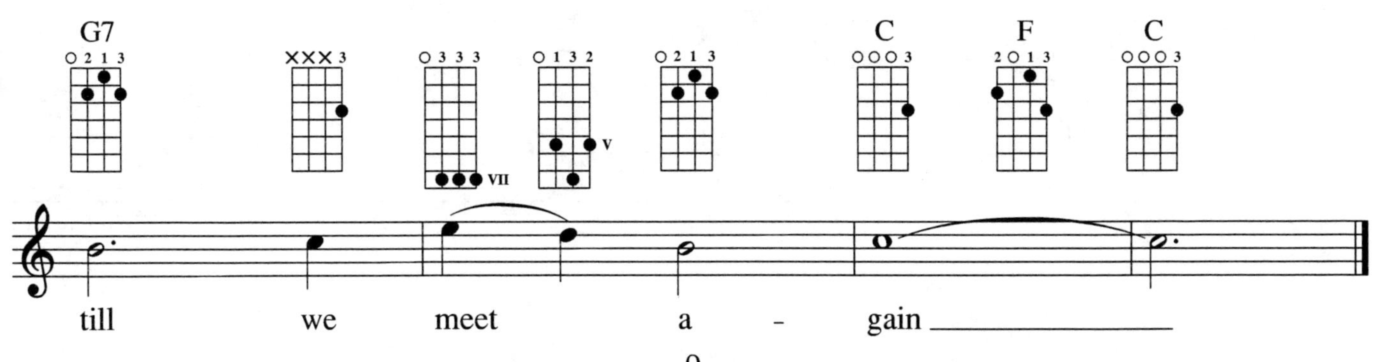

G7
C
F
C
till we meet a - gain

disc
3

JA - DA

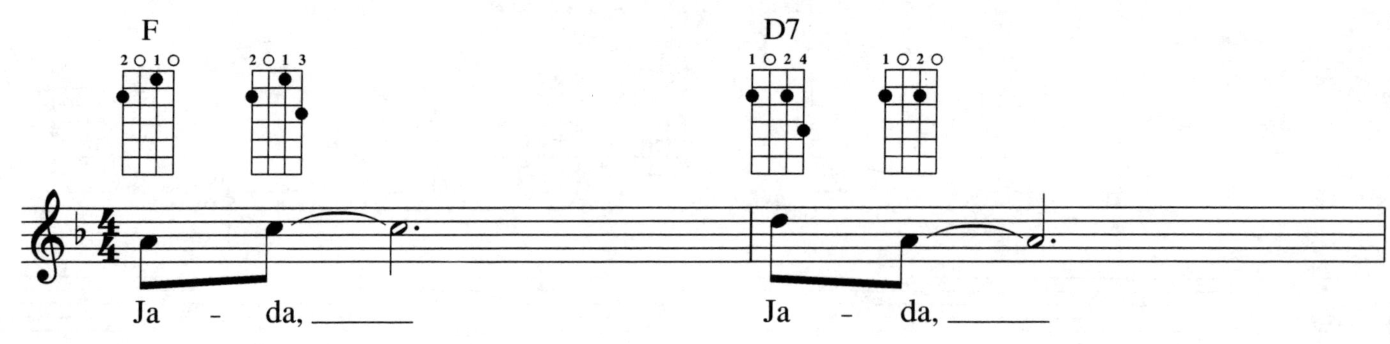
F
D7
Ja - da,
Ja - da,

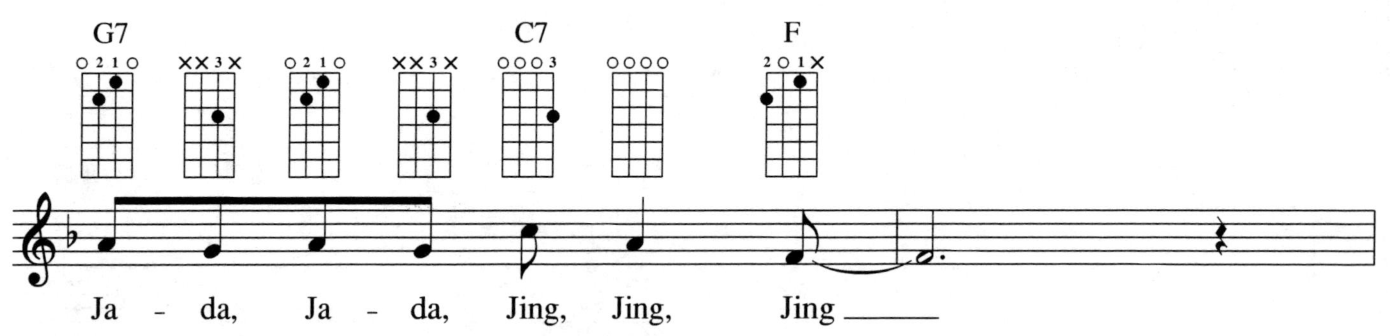
G7
C7
F
Ja - da, Ja - da, Jing, Jing, Jing

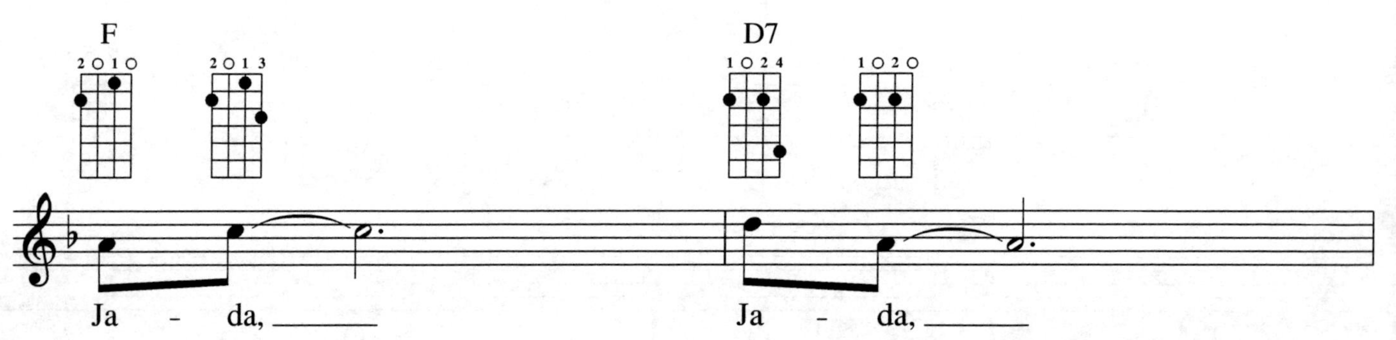
F
D7
Ja - da,
Ja - da,

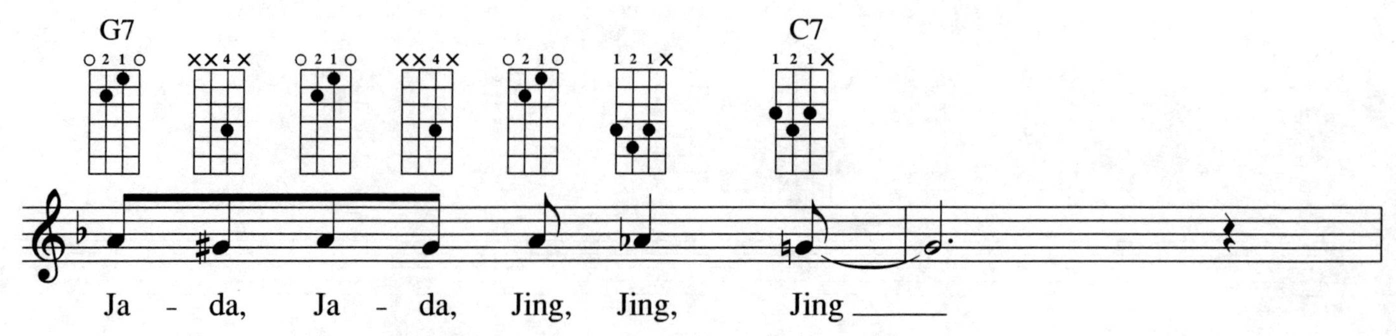
G7
C7
Ja - da, Ja - da, Jing, Jing, Jing

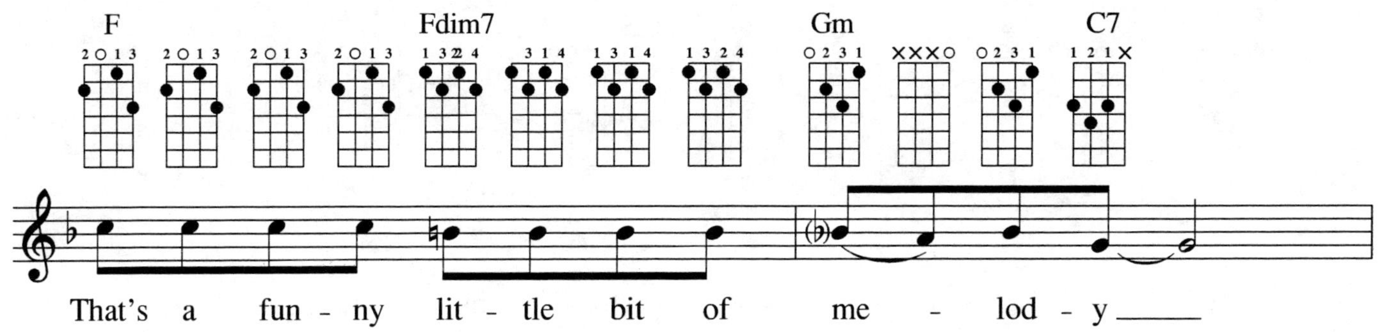
F
Fdim7
Gm
C7
That's a fun - ny lit - tle bit of me - lod - y

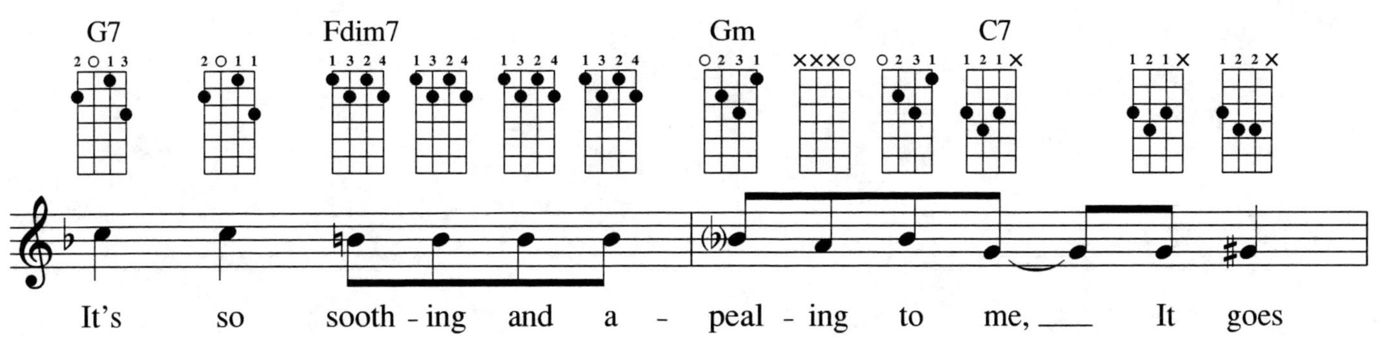
G7
Fdim7
Gm
C7
It's so sooth - ing and a - peal - ing to me, It goes

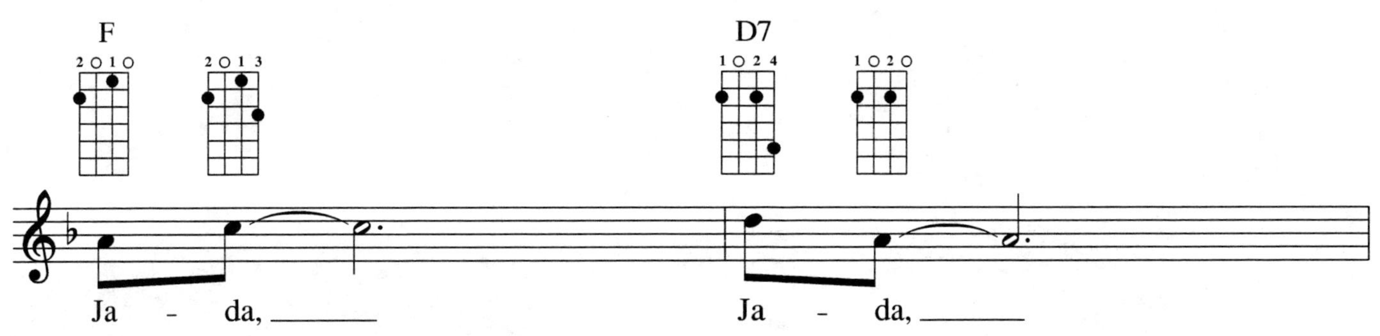
F
D7
Ja - da,
Ja - da,

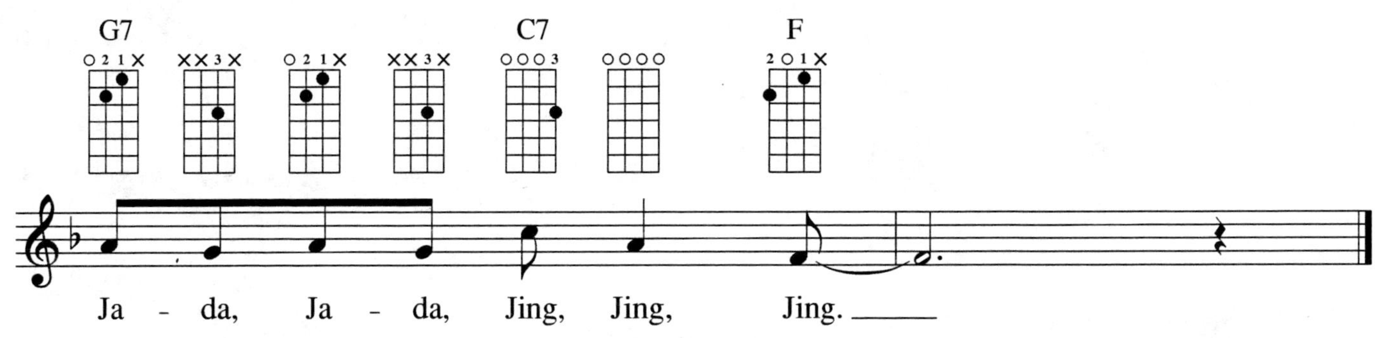
G7
C7
F
Ja - da, Ja - da, Jing, Jing, Jing.

CHINATOWN, MY CHINATOWN

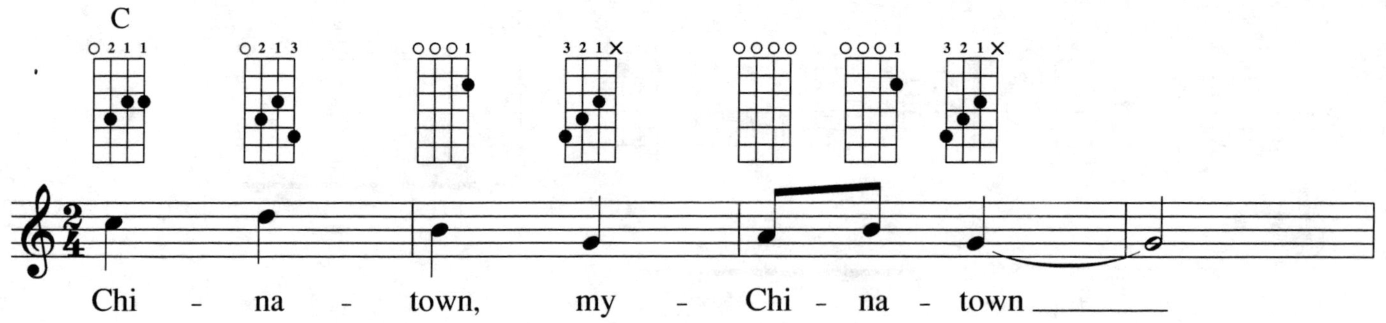
C
Chi - na - town, my - Chi - na - town

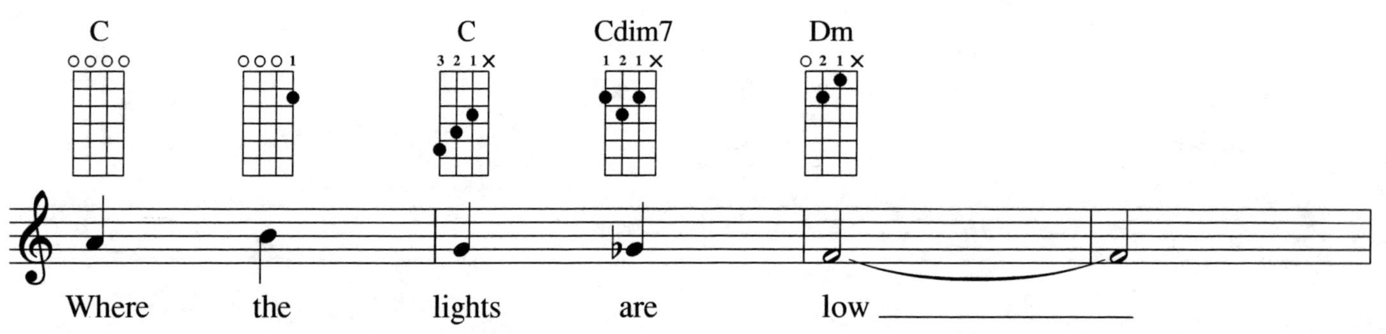
C
C
Cdim7
Dm
Where the lights are low

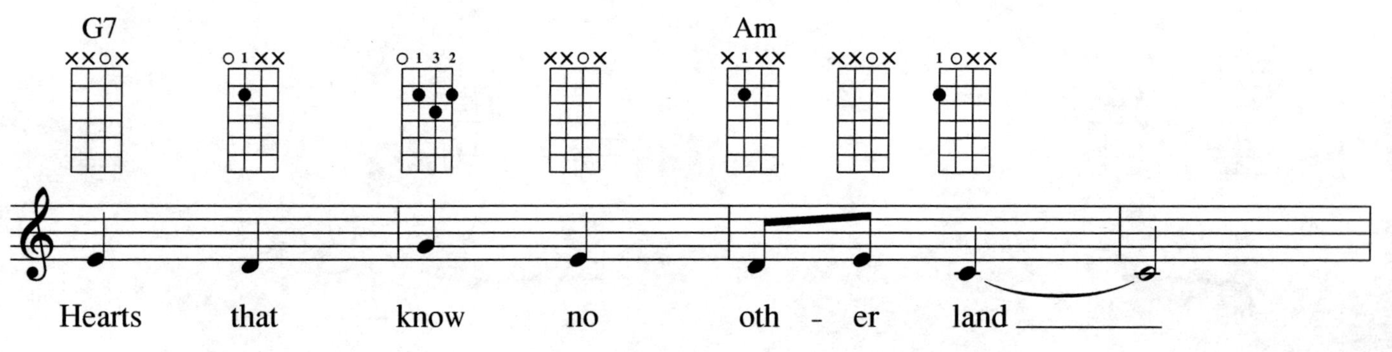
G7
Am
Hearts that know no oth - er land

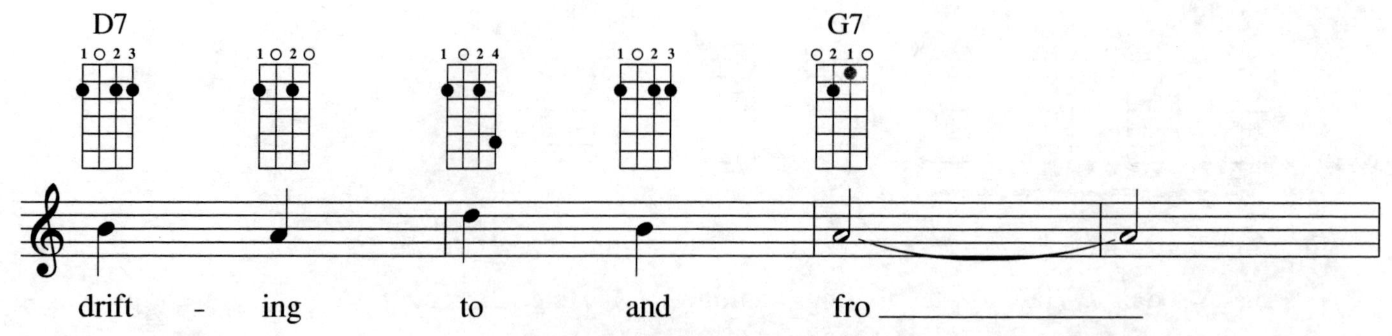
D7
G7
drift - ing to and fro

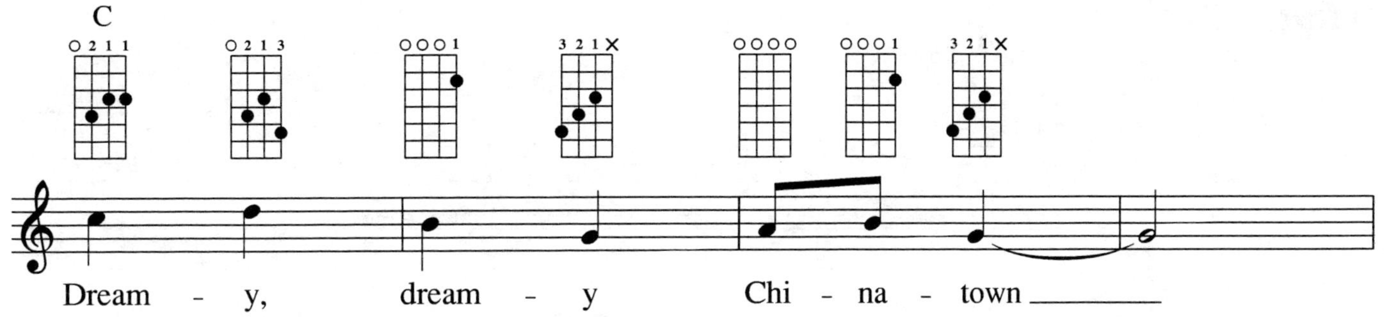
C
Dream - y, dream - y Chi - na - town

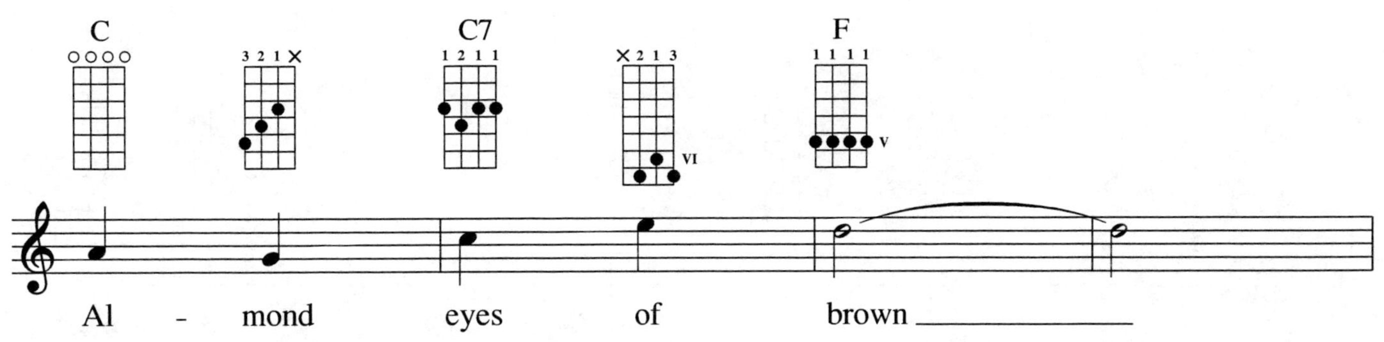
C
C7
F
Al - mond eyes of brown

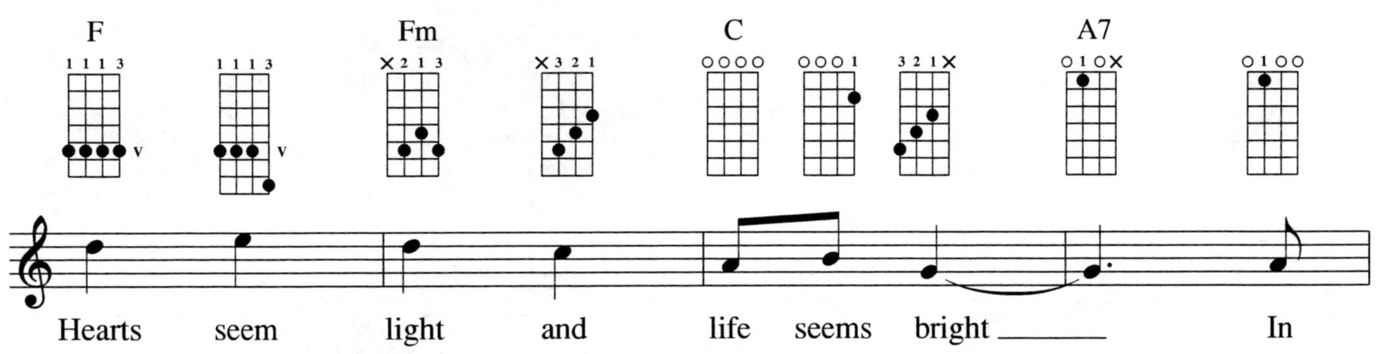
F
Fm
C
A7
Hearts seem light and life seems bright In

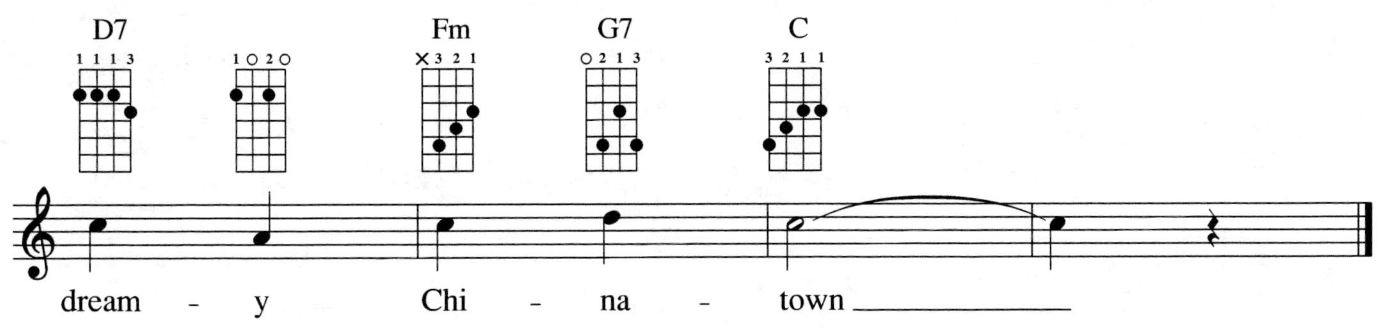
D7
Fm
G7
C
dream - y Chi - na - town

WHEN THE SAINTS GO MARCHING IN

5

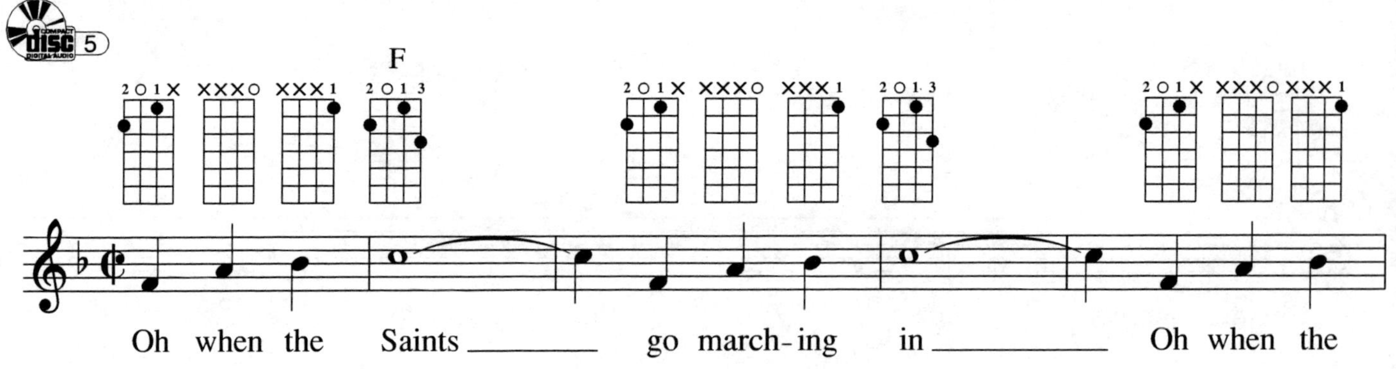
F
2 0 1 X
X X X 0
X X X 1
2 0 1 3
2 0 1 X
X X X 0
X X X 1
2 0 1 3
2 0 1 X
X X X 0
X X X 1
Oh when the Saints ____ go march-ing in ____ Oh when the

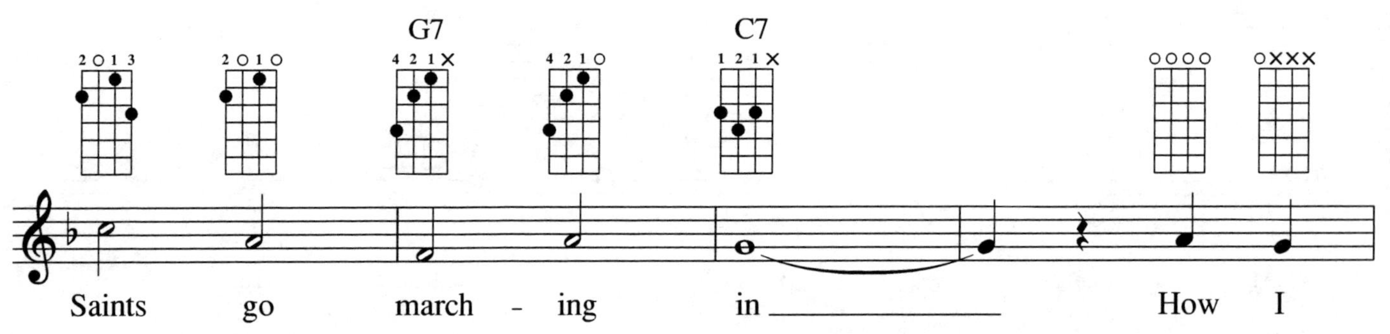
G7
C7
2 0 1 3
2 0 1 0
4 2 1 X
4 2 1 0
1 2 1 X
0 0 0 0
0 X X X
Saints go march - ing in ____ How I

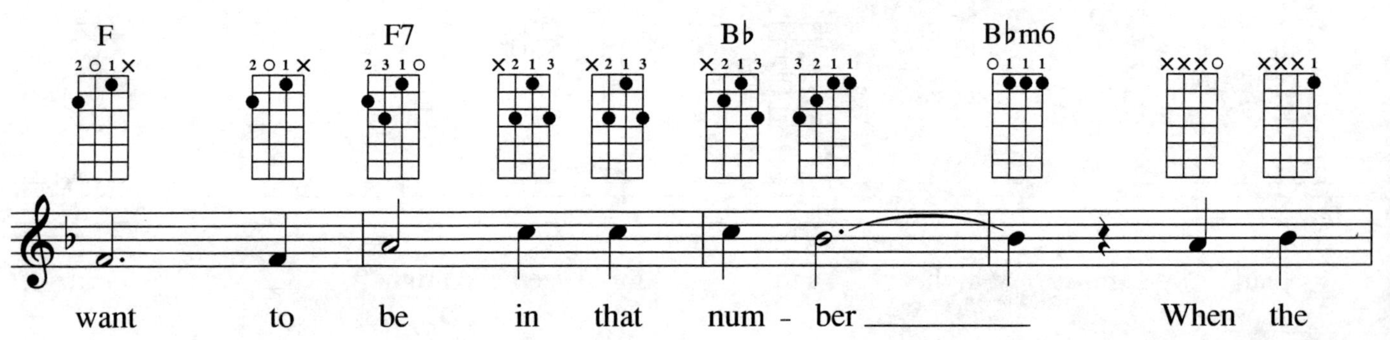
F
F7
B♭
B♭m6
2 0 1 X
2 0 1 X
2 3 1 0
X 2 1 3
X 2 1 3
X 2 1 3
3 2 1 1
0 1 1 1
X X X 0
X X X 1
want to be in that num - ber ____ When the

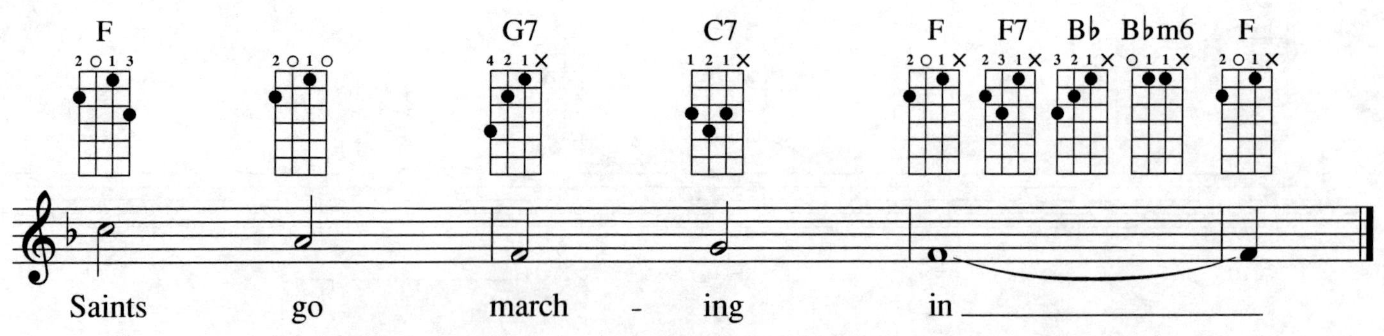
F
G7
C7
F
F7
B♭
B♭m6
F
2 0 1 3
2 0 1 0
4 2 1 X
1 2 1 X
2 0 1 X
2 3 1 X
3 2 1 X
0 1 1 X
2 0 1 X
Saints go march - ing in ____

SONG OF THE ISLANDS

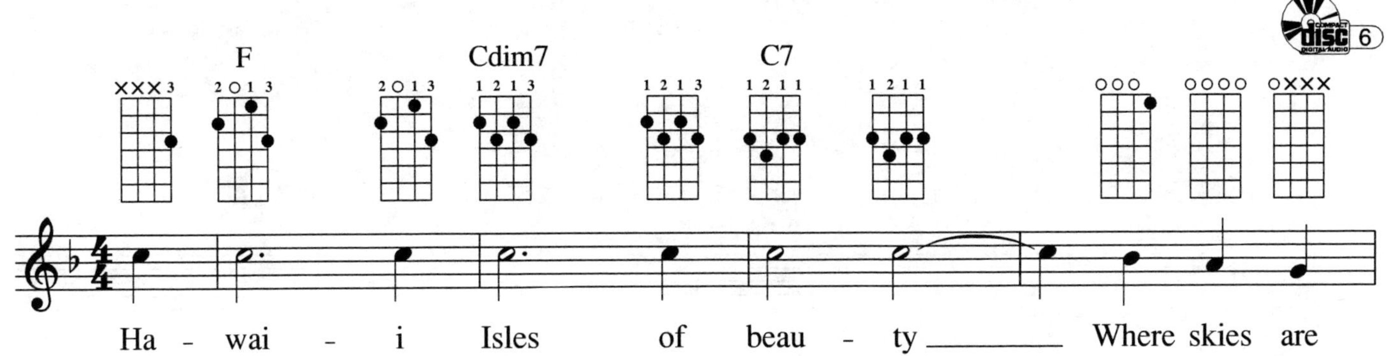
6
F
Cdim7
C7
Ha - wai - i Isles of beau - ty Where skies are

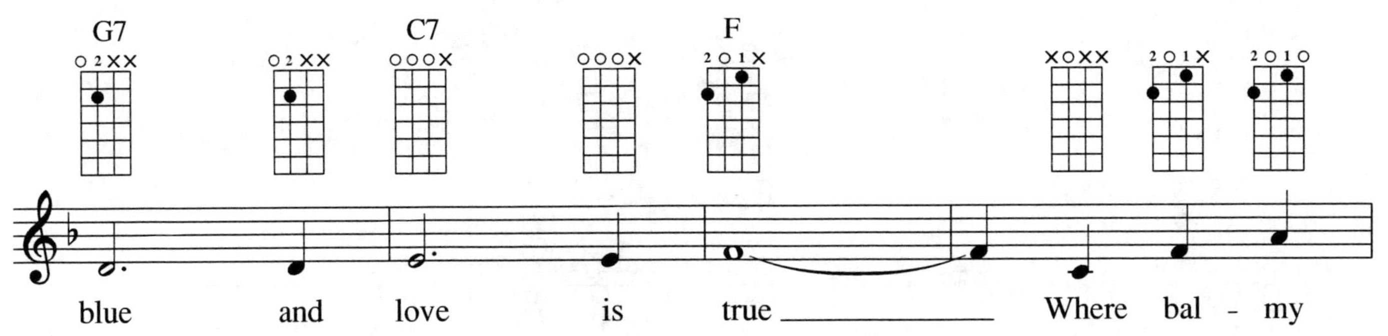
G7
C7
F
blue and love is true Where bal - my

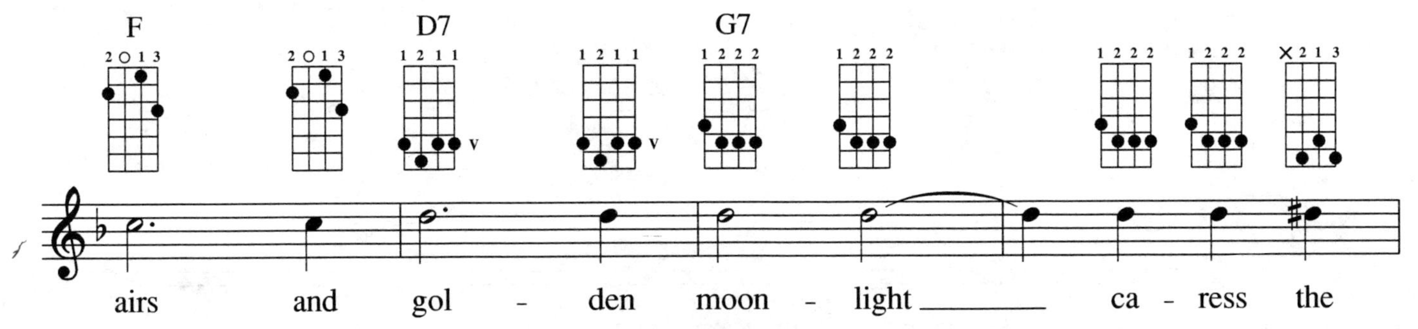
F
D7
G7
airs and gol - den moon - light ca - ress the

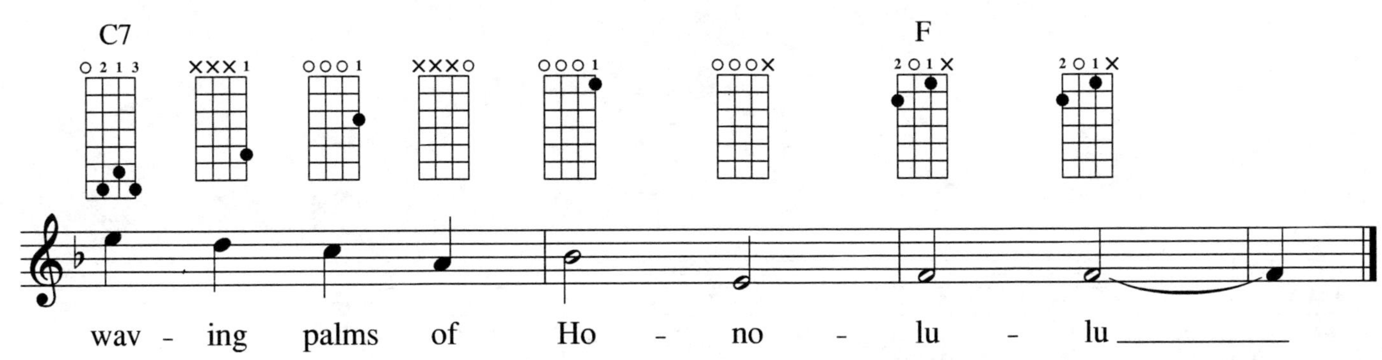
C7
F
wav - ing palms of Ho - no - lu - lu

YOU TELL ME YOUR DREAM, I'LL TELL YOU MINE

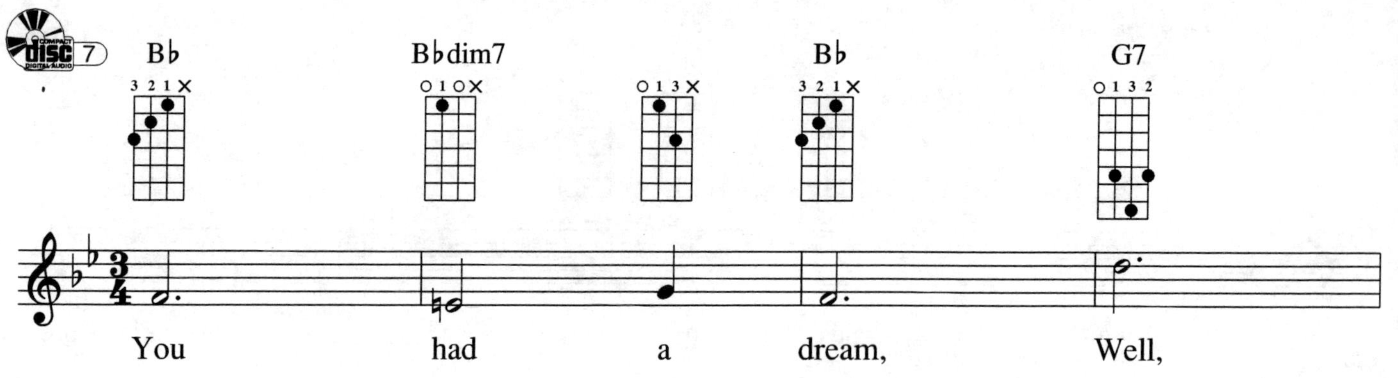
7
B♭
B♭dim7
B♭
G7
You had a dream,
Well,

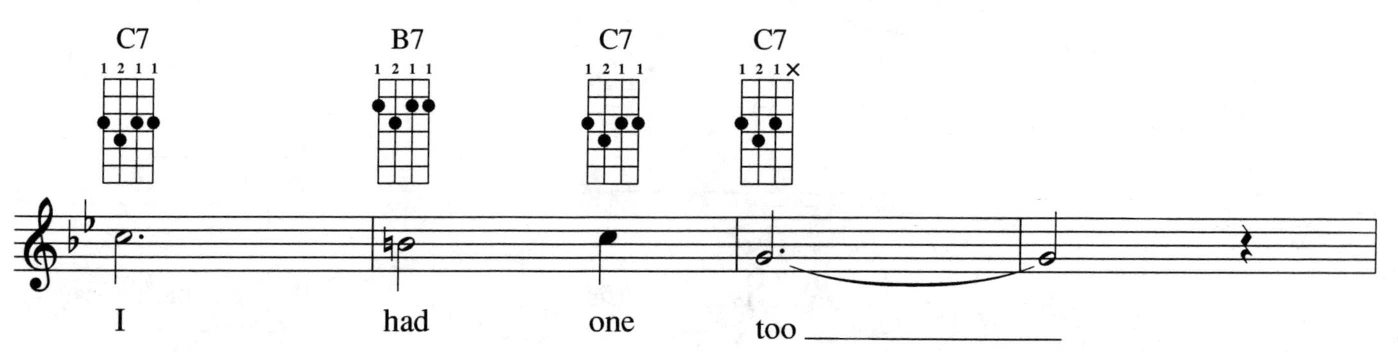
C7
B7
C7
C7
I had one too

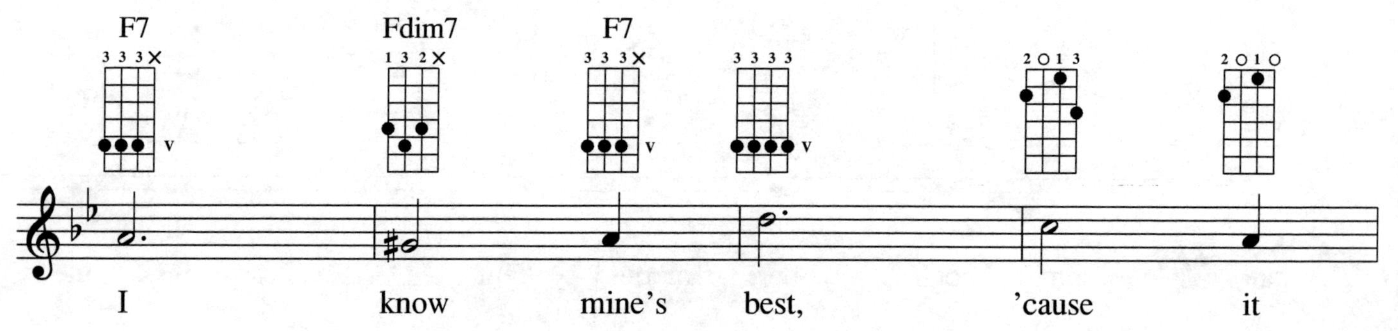
F7
Fdim7
F7
I know mine's best,
'cause it

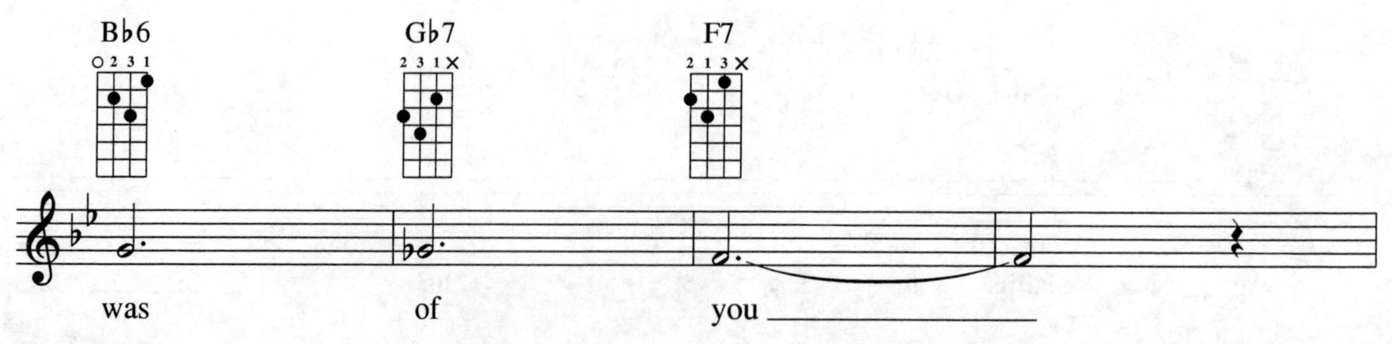
B♭6
G♭7
F7
was of you

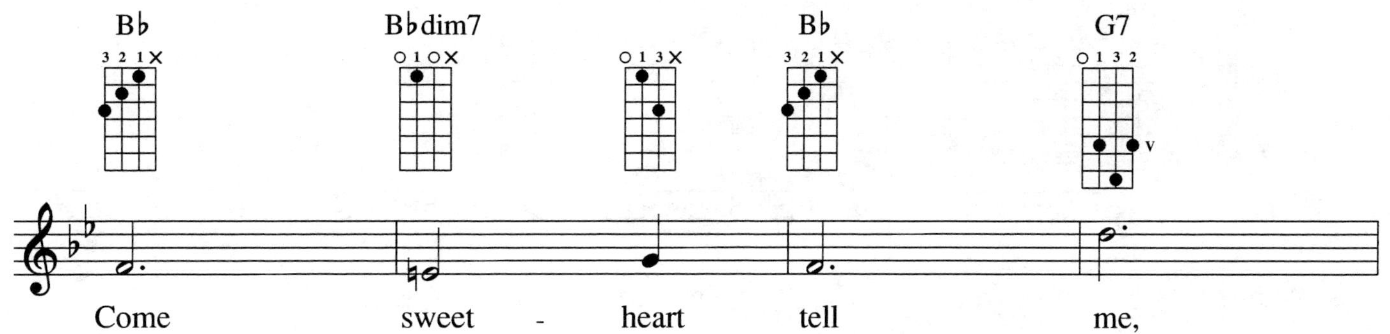
B♭
B♭dim7
B♭
G7
Come sweet - heart tell me,

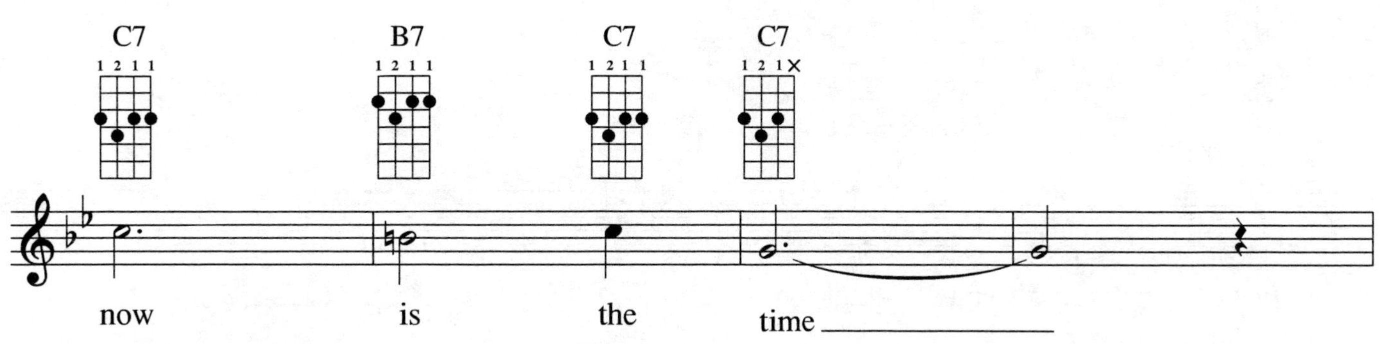
C7
B7
C7
C7
now is the time

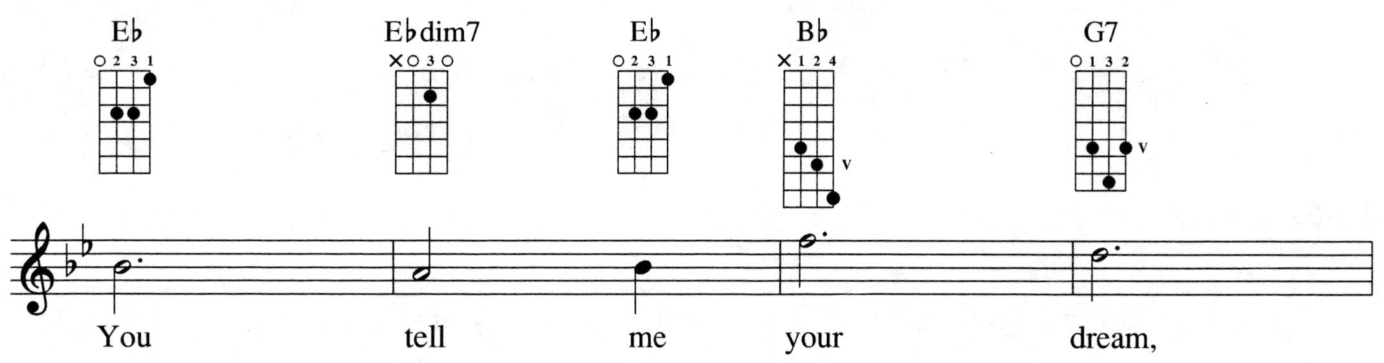
E♭
E♭dim7
E♭
B♭
G7
You tell me your dream,

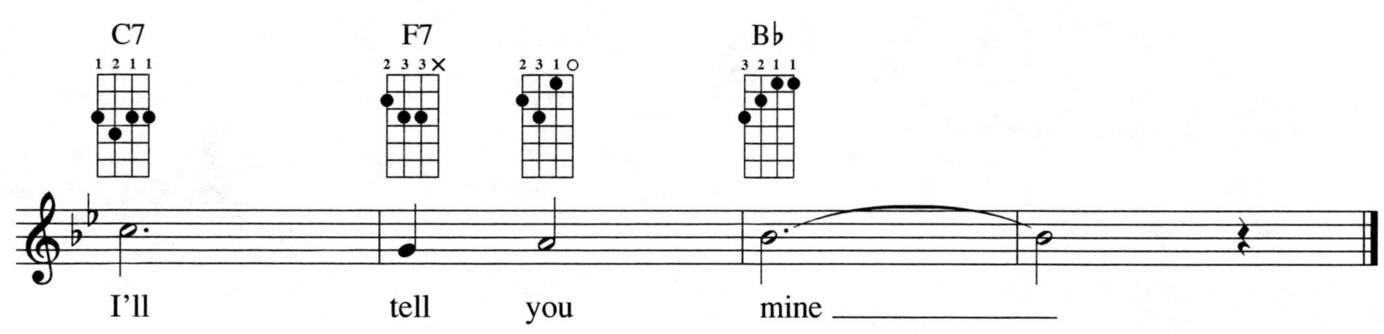
C7
F7
B♭
I'll tell you mine

disc
8

JUST BECAUSE

C
Just be-cause you think you're so pret - ty

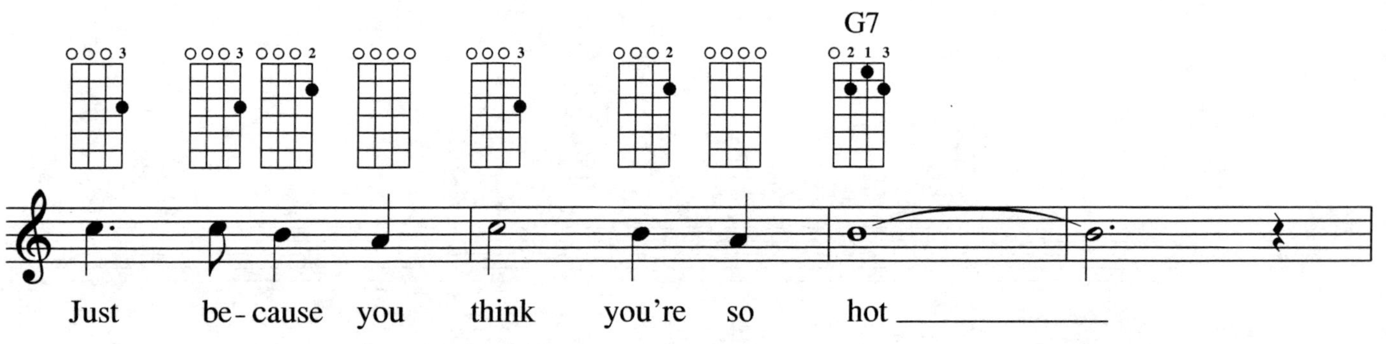
G7
Just be-cause you think you're so hot

Just be-cause you think you've got some - thing that

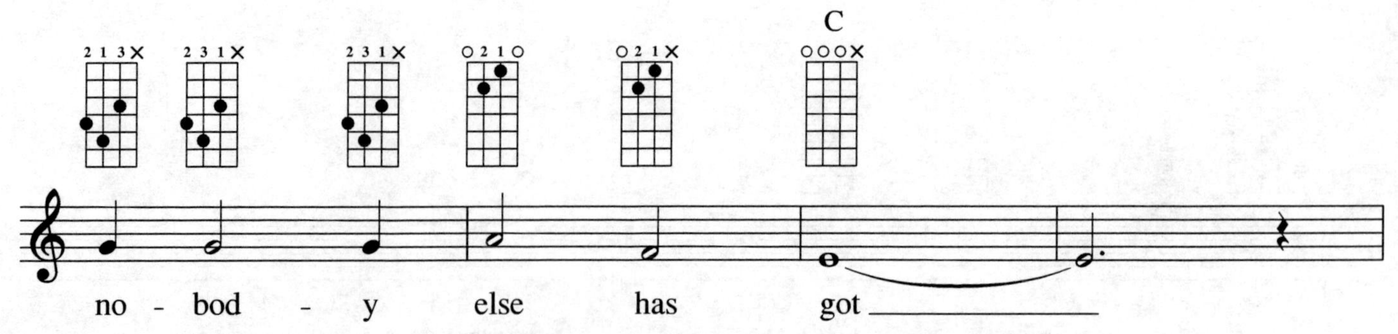
C
no - bod - y else has got

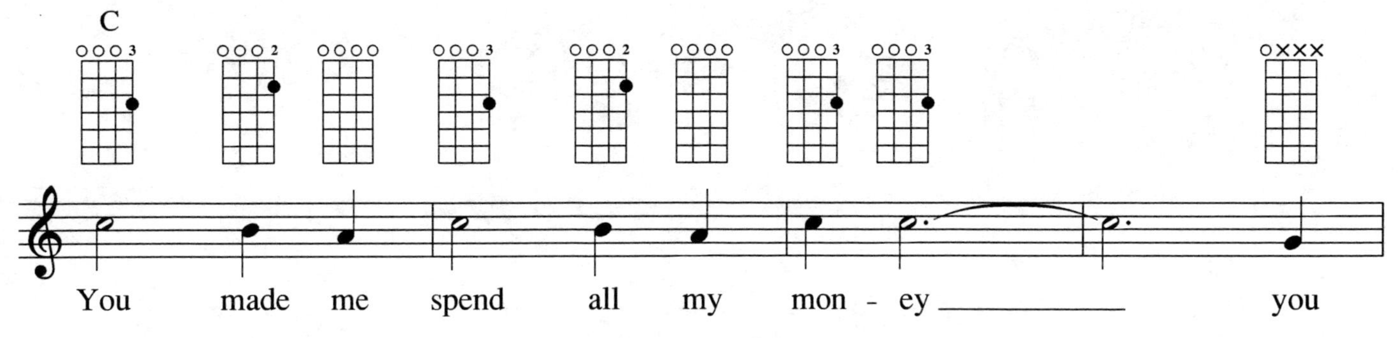
C
You made me spend all my mon - ey you

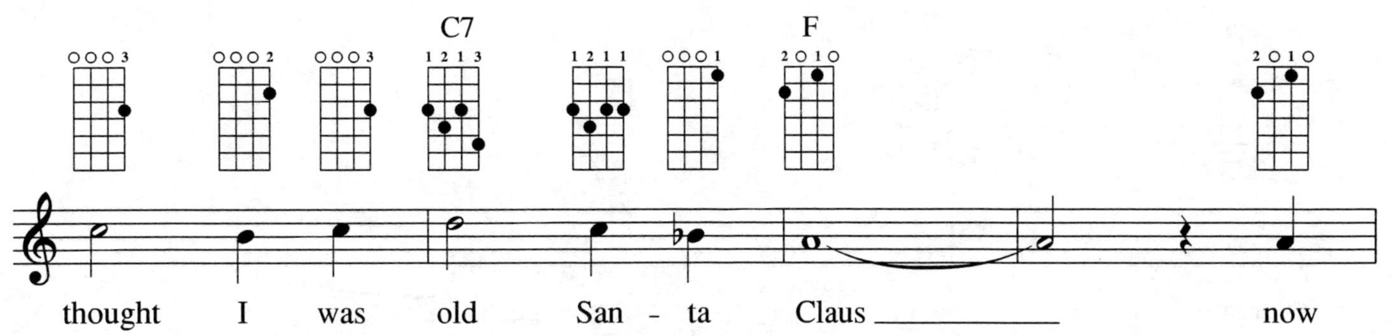
C7
F
thought I was old San - ta Claus now

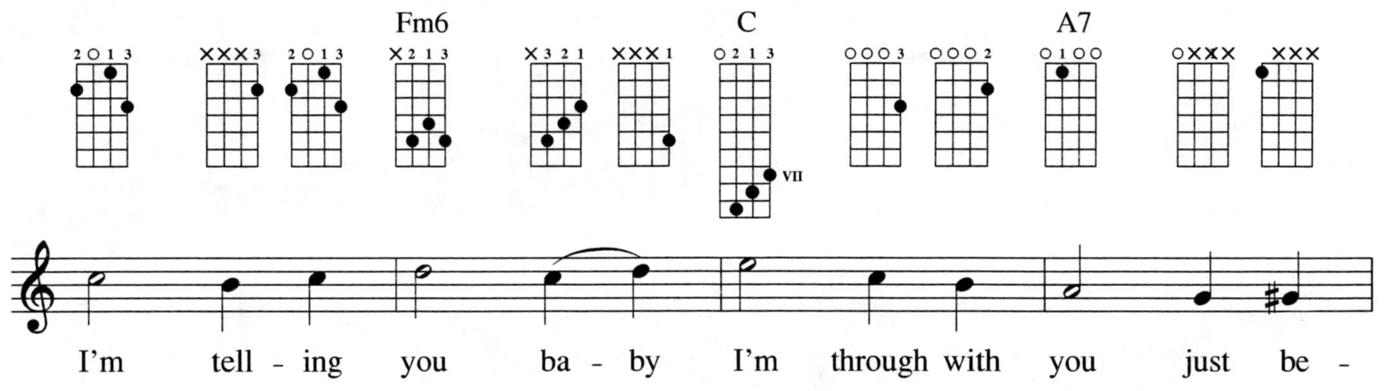
Fm6
C
A7
VII
I'm tell - ing you ba - by I'm through with you just be -

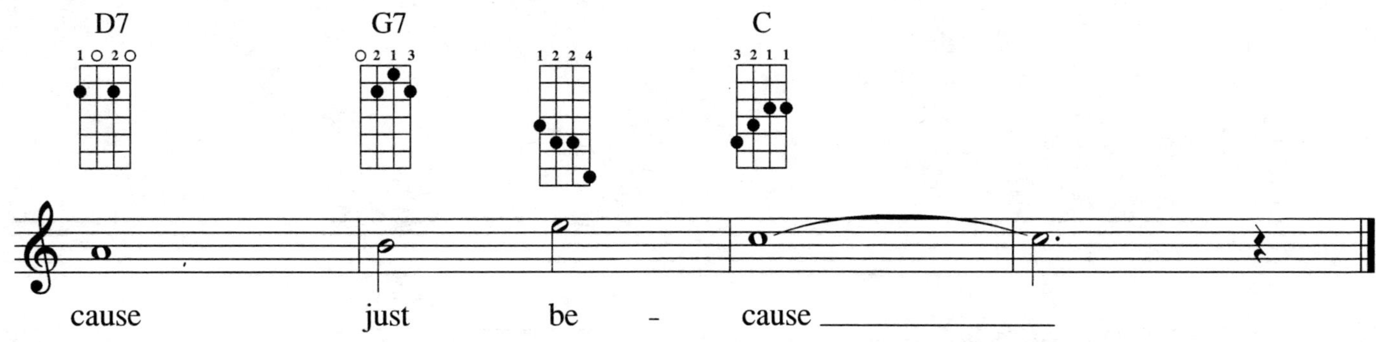
D7
G7
C
cause just be - cause

disc
9

MELODY OF LOVE

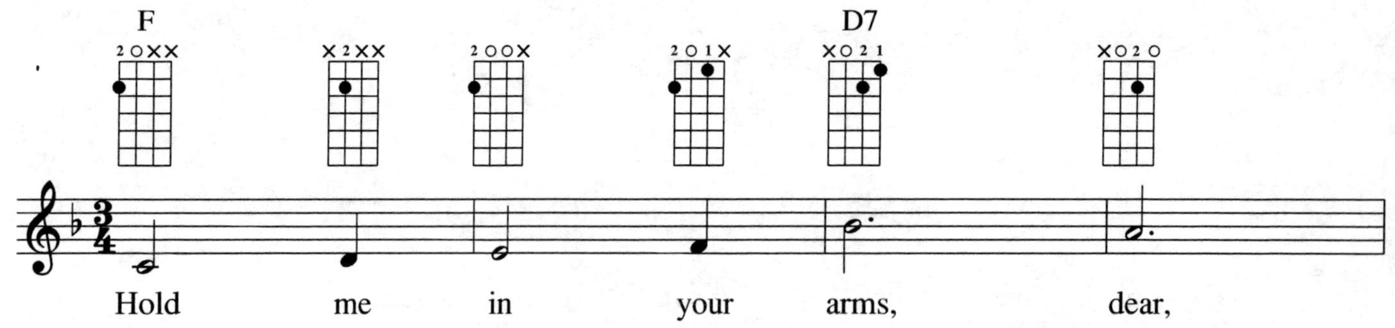
F
D7
Hold me in your arms, dear,

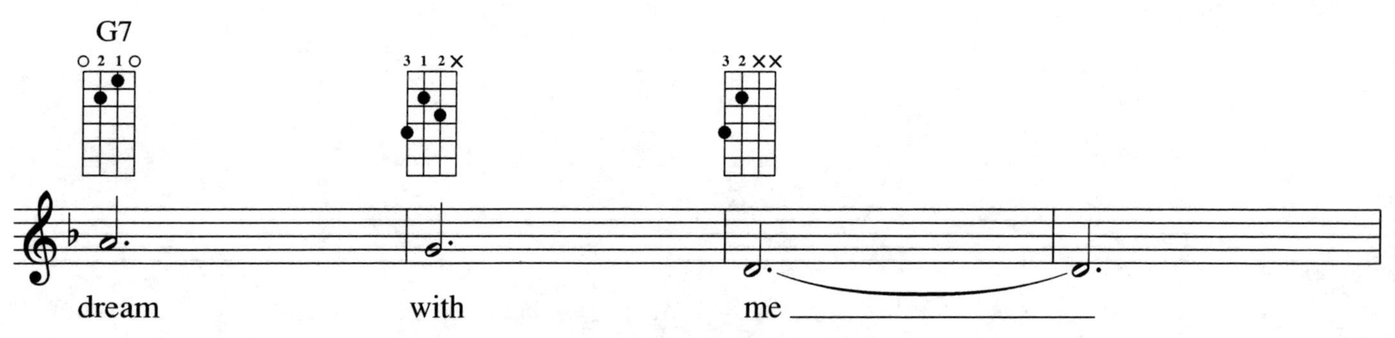
G7
dream with me

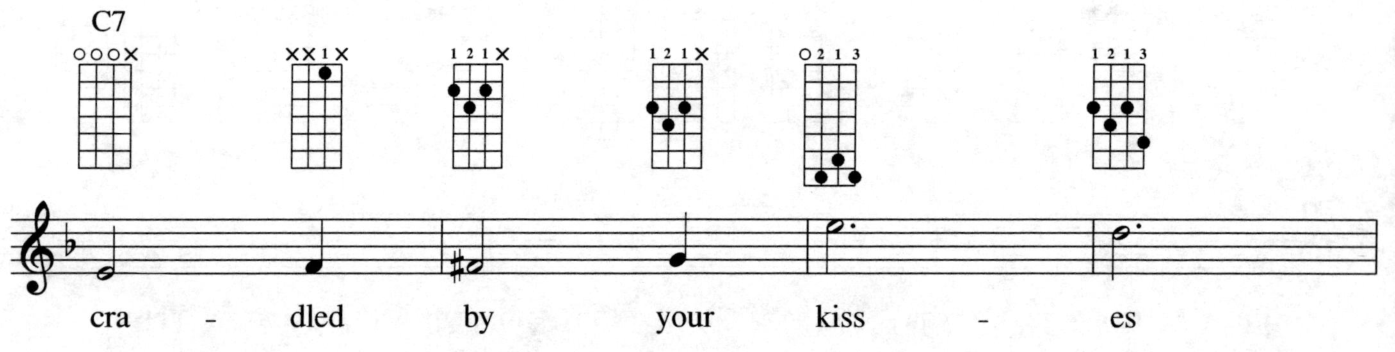
C7
cra - dled by your kiss - es

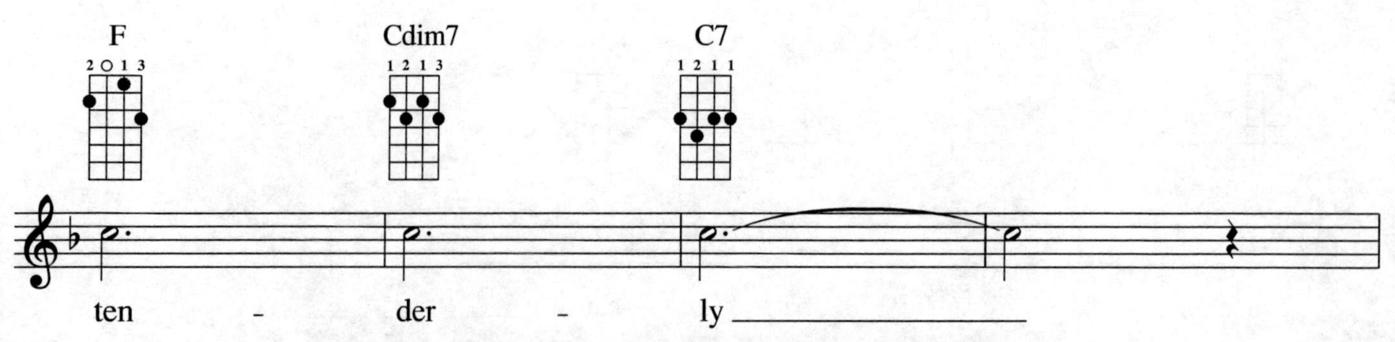
F
Cdim7
C7
ten - der - ly

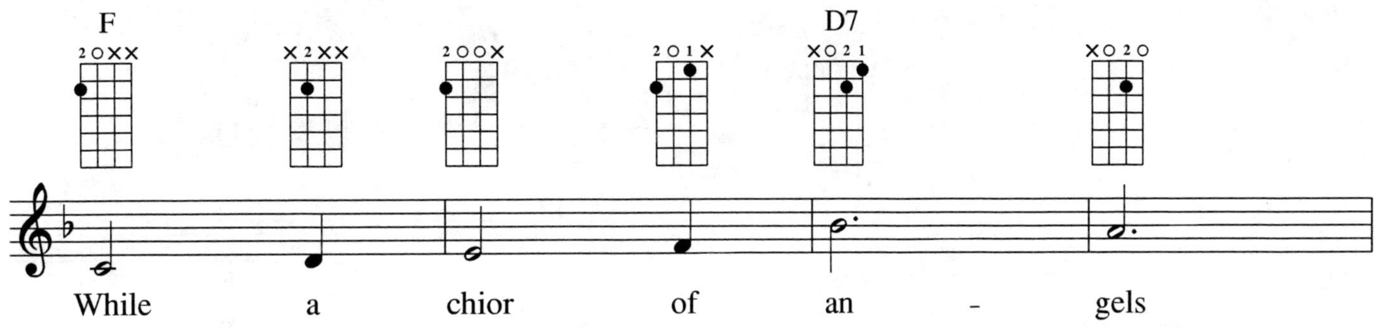
F
D7
While a chior of an - gels

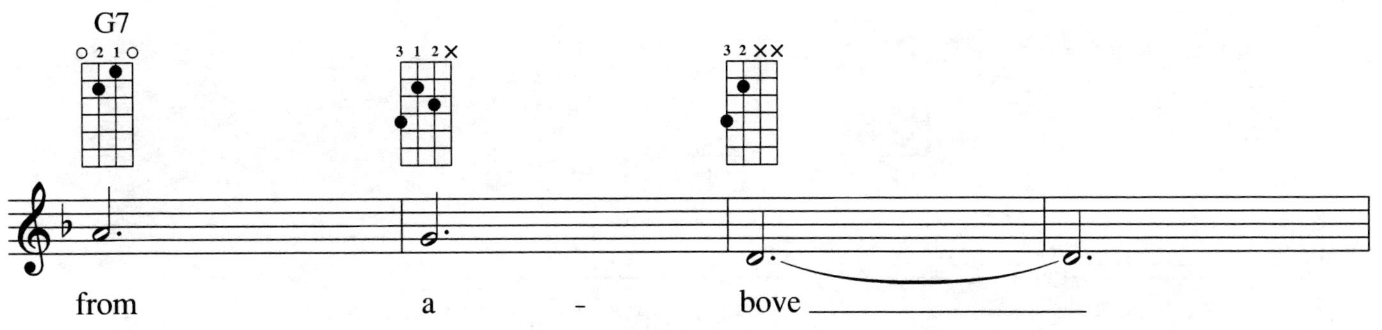
G7
from a - bove

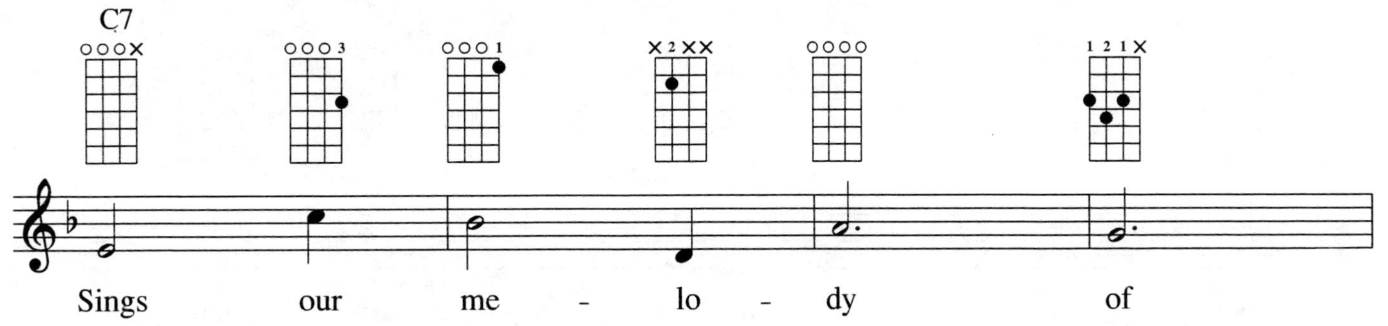
C7
Sings our me - lo - dy of

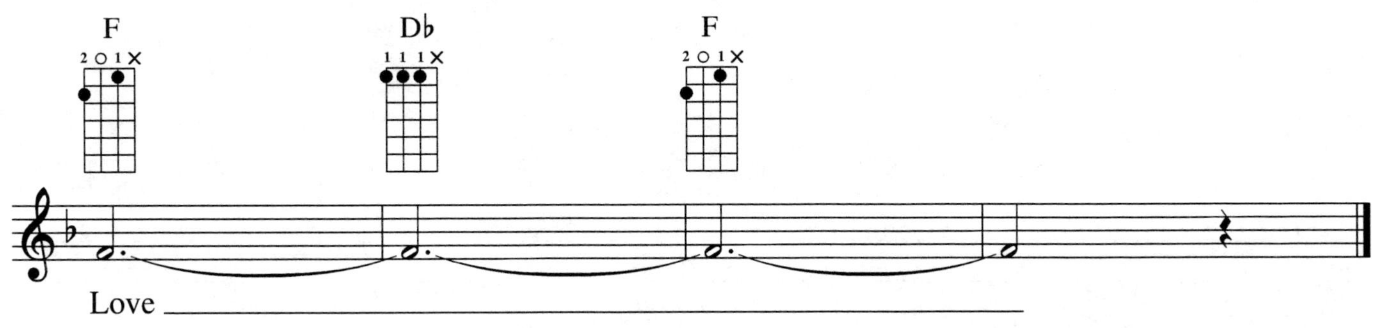
F
D♭
F
Love

SWEETHEART OF SIGMA CHI

10

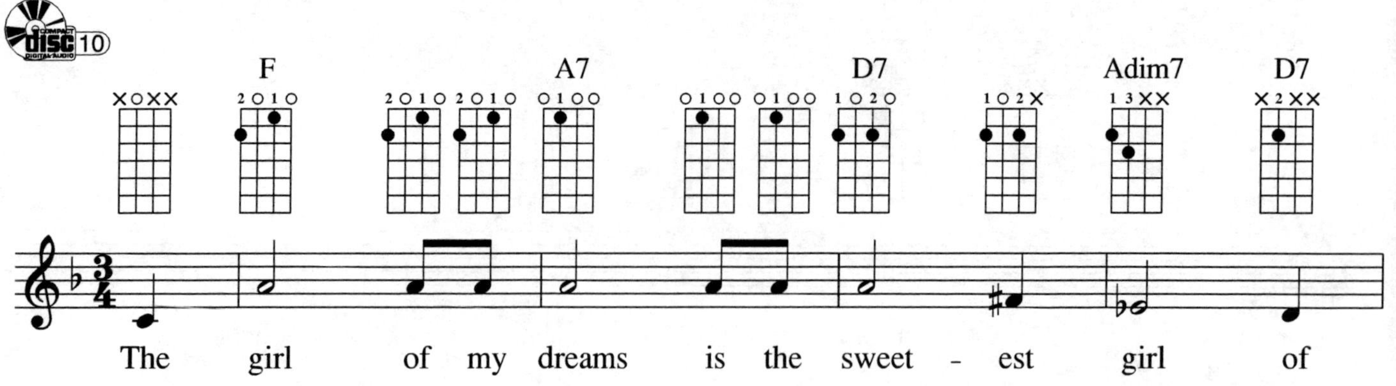
F A7 D7 Adim7 D7
The girl of my dreams is the sweet - est girl of

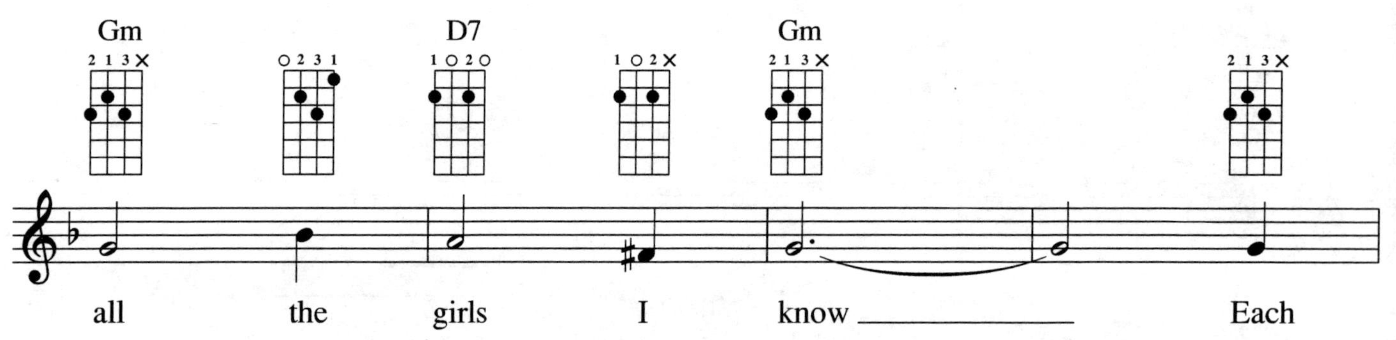
Gm D7 Gm
all the girls I know Each

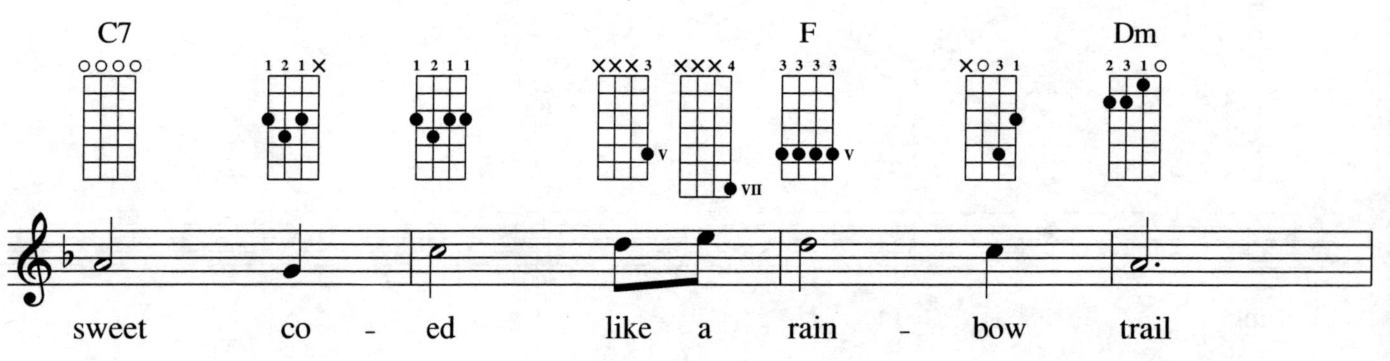
C7 F Dm
sweet co - ed like a rain - bow trail

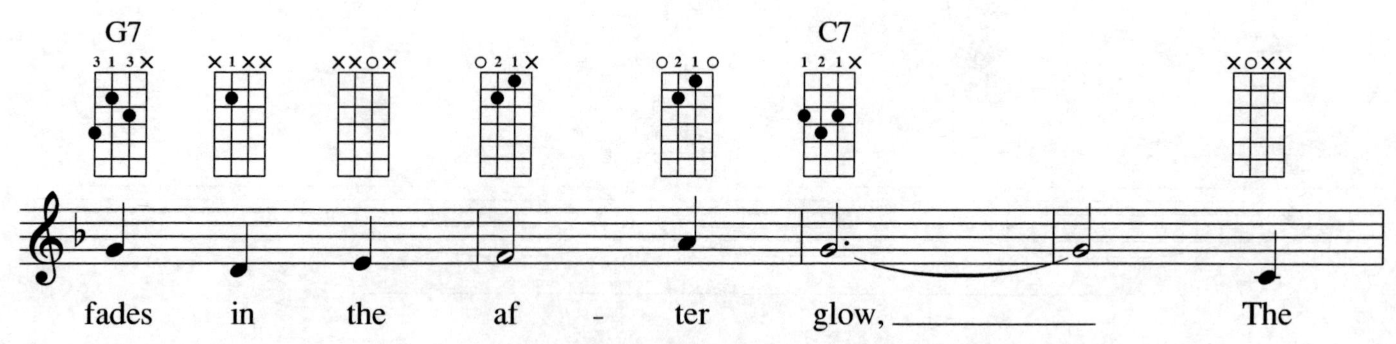
G7 C7
fades in the af - ter glow, The

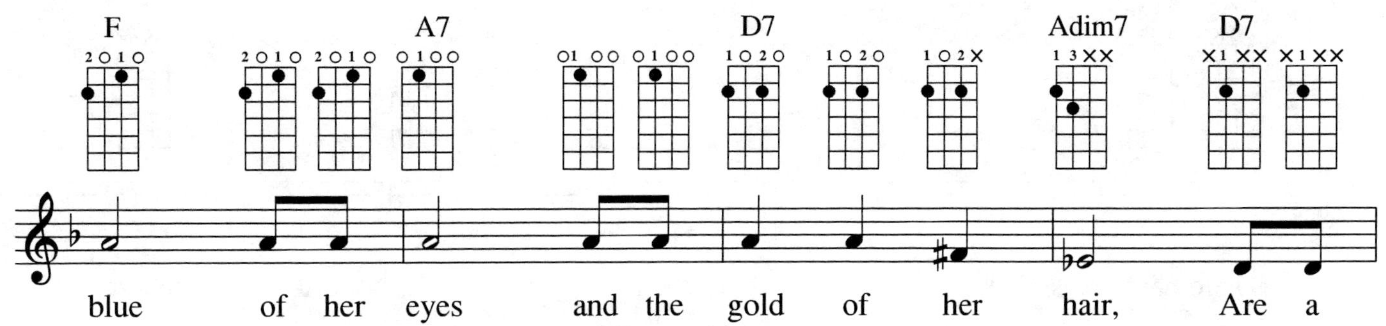
F A7 D7 Adim7 D7
blue of her eyes and the gold of her hair, Are a

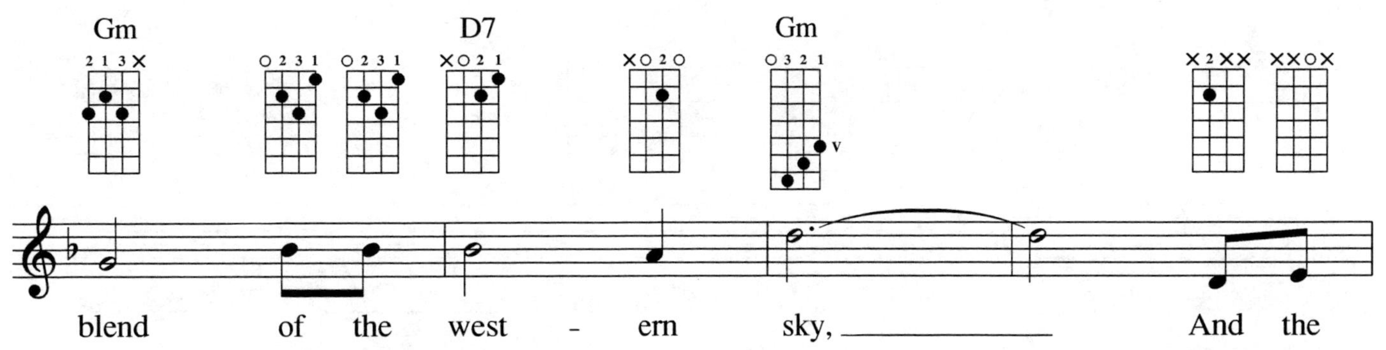
Gm D7 Gm
blend of the west - ern sky, And the

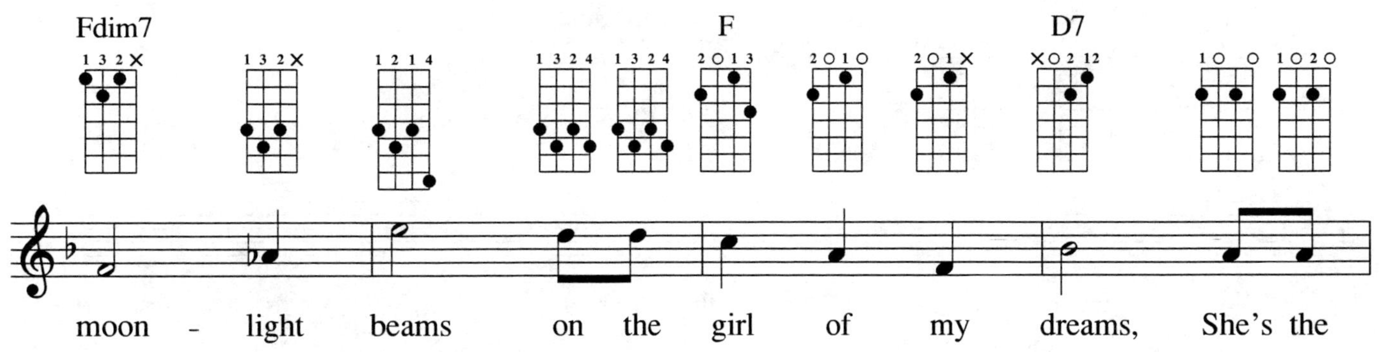
Fdim7 F D7
moon - light beams on the girl of my dreams, She's the

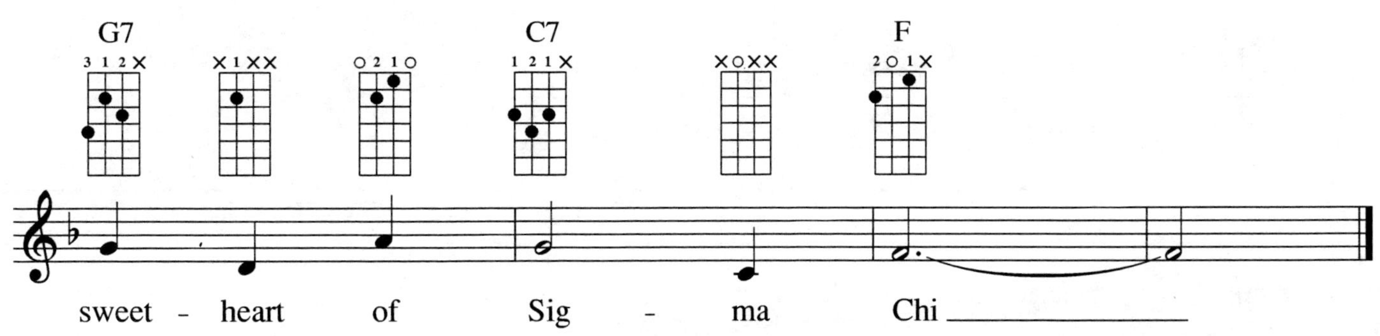
G7 C7 F
sweet - heart of Sig - ma Chi

disc
11

SMILES

C7
Gm7 C7
There are smiles that make us hap - py, There are

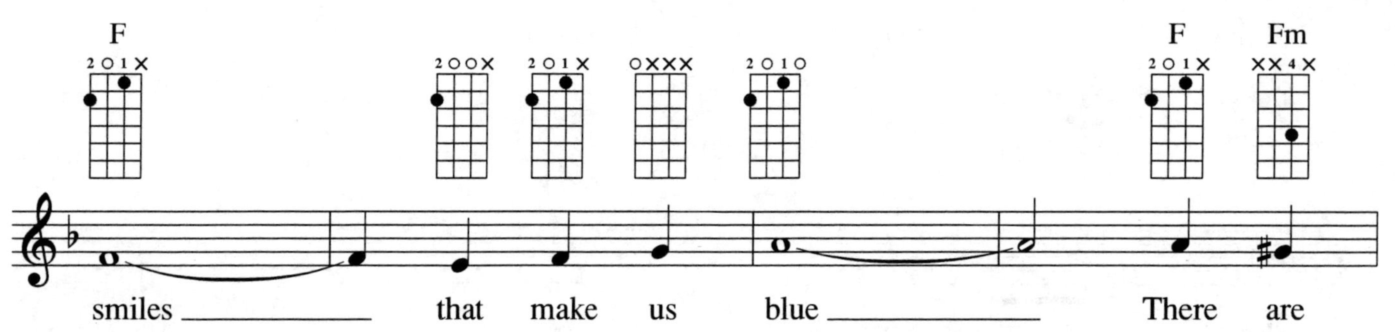
F
F Fm
smiles that make us blue There are

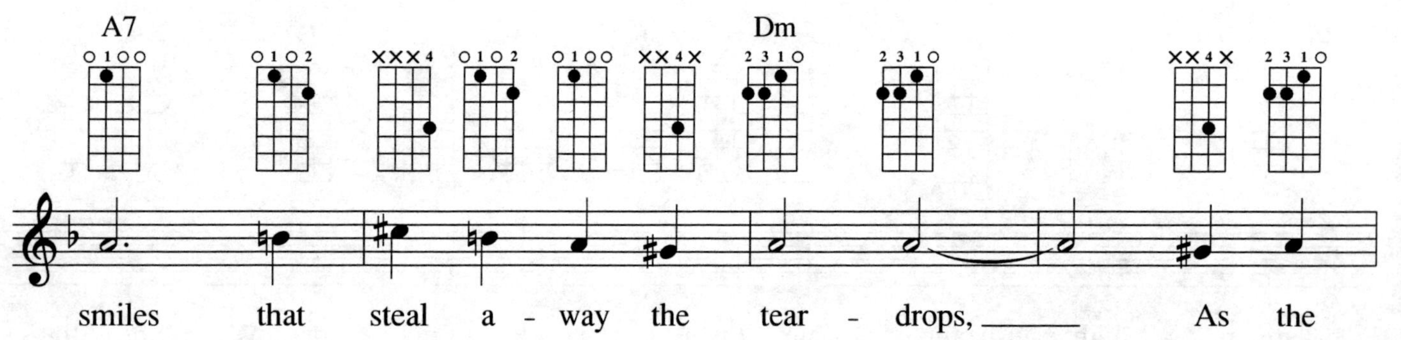
A7
Dm
smiles that steal a - way the tear - drops, As the

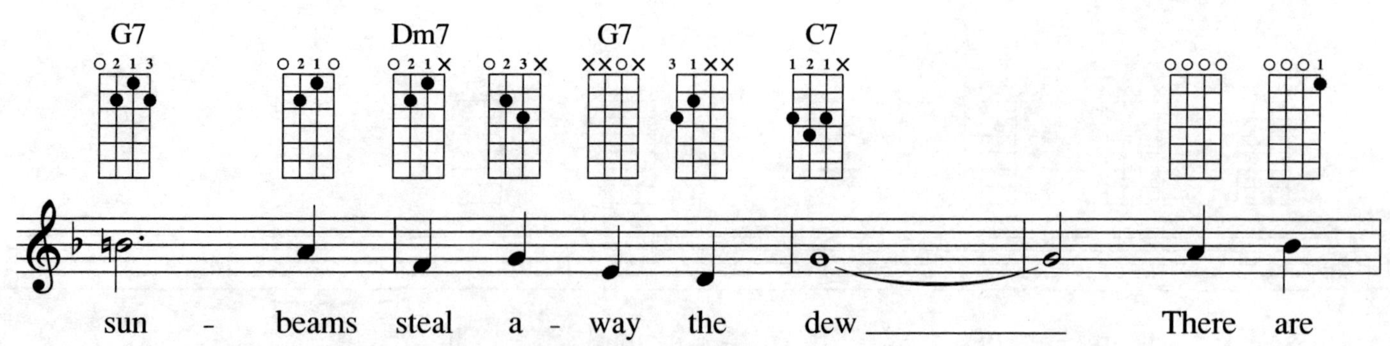
G7
Dm7
G7
C7
sun - beams steal a - way the dew There are

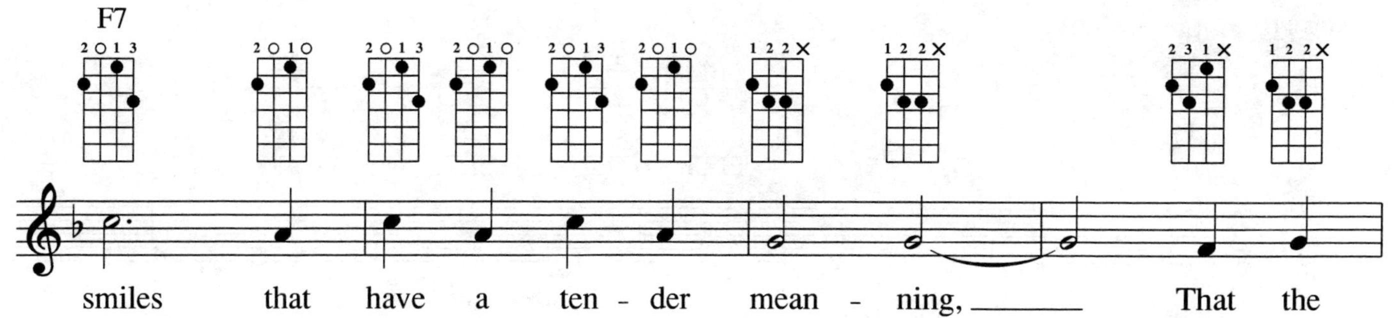
F7
smiles that have a ten - der mean - ning, That the

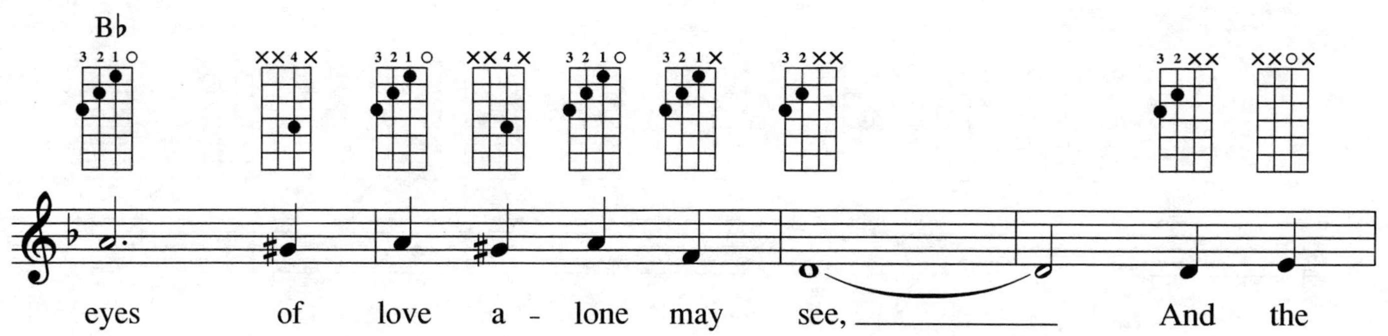
B♭
eyes of love a - lone may see, And the

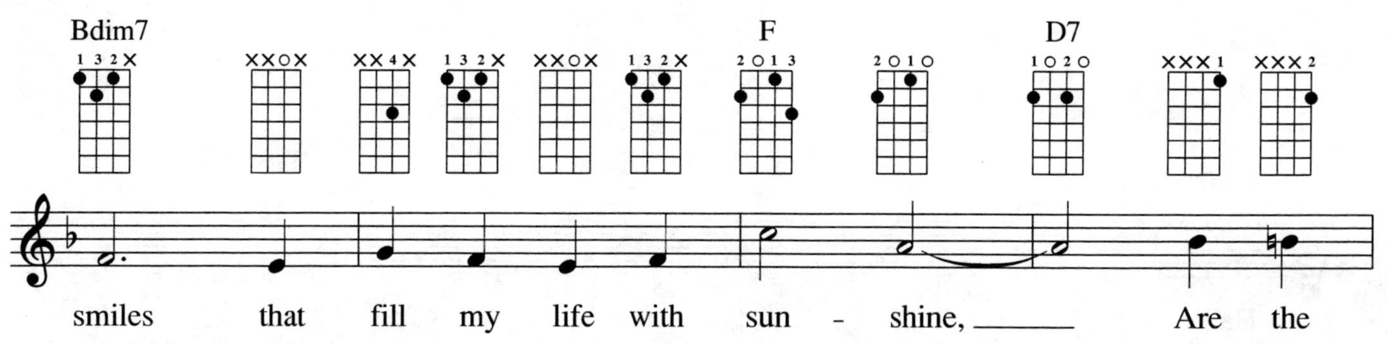
Bdim7
F
D7
smiles that fill my life with sun - shine, Are the

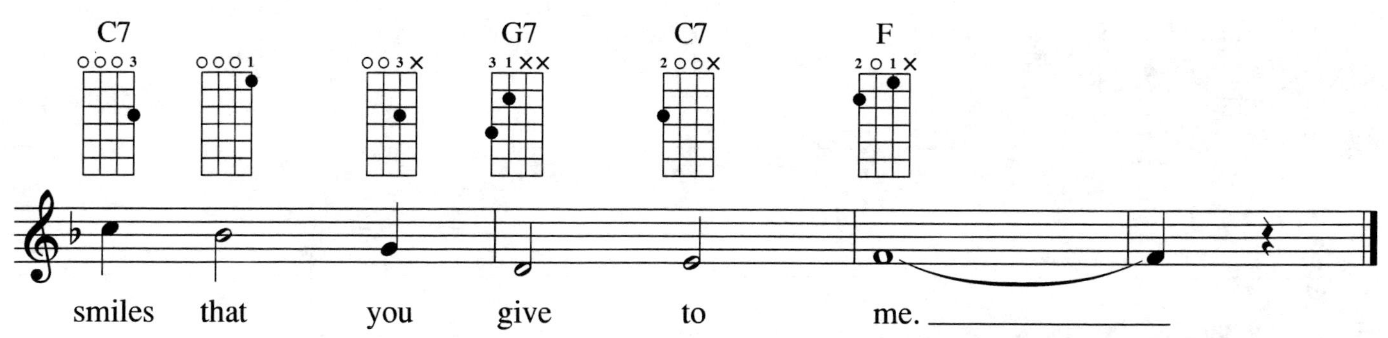
C7
G7
C7
F
smiles that you give to me.

HAIL, HAIL THE GANG'S ALL HERE

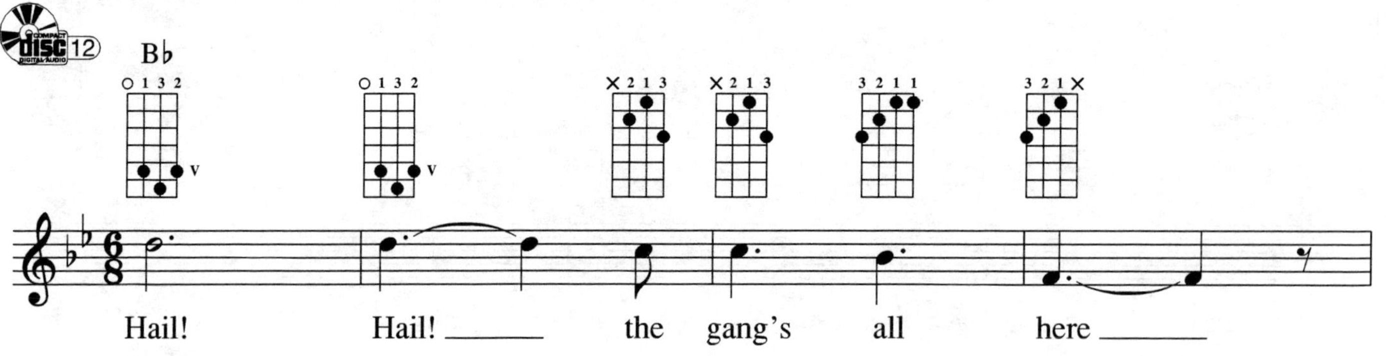

Bb
Hail! Hail! the gang's all here

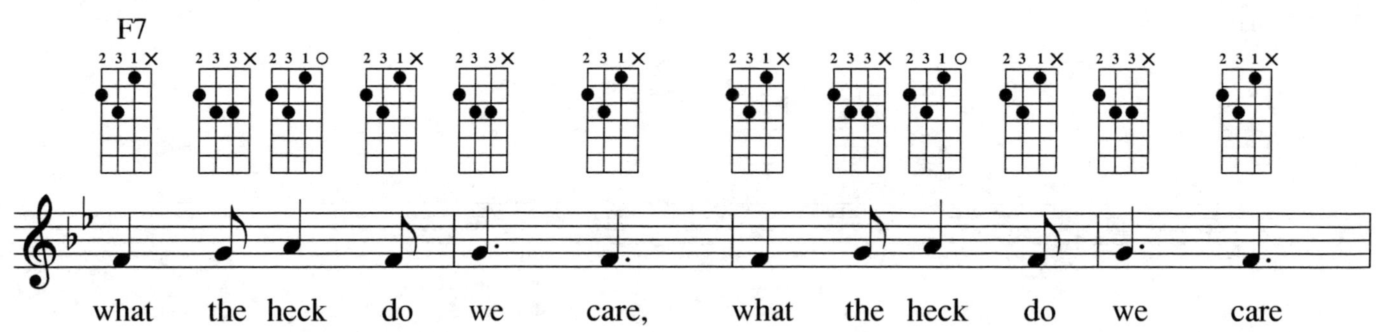

F7
what the heck do we care, what the heck do we care

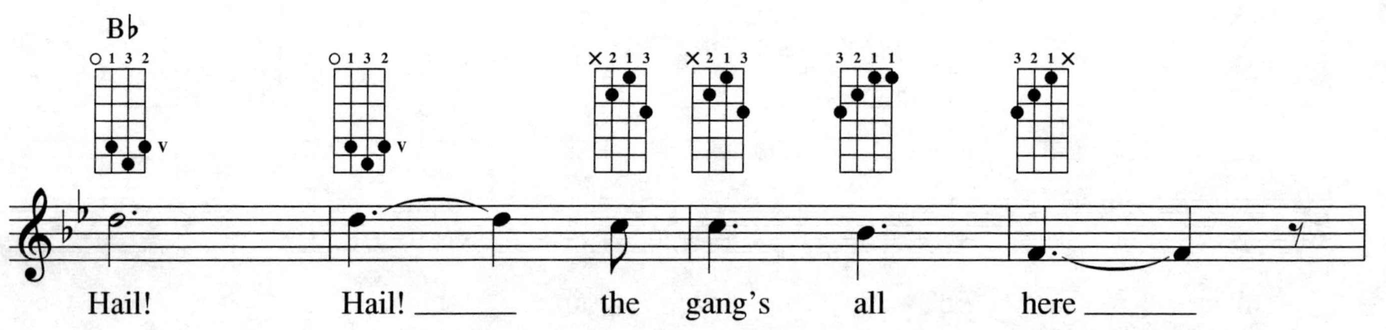

Bb
Hail! Hail! the gang's all here

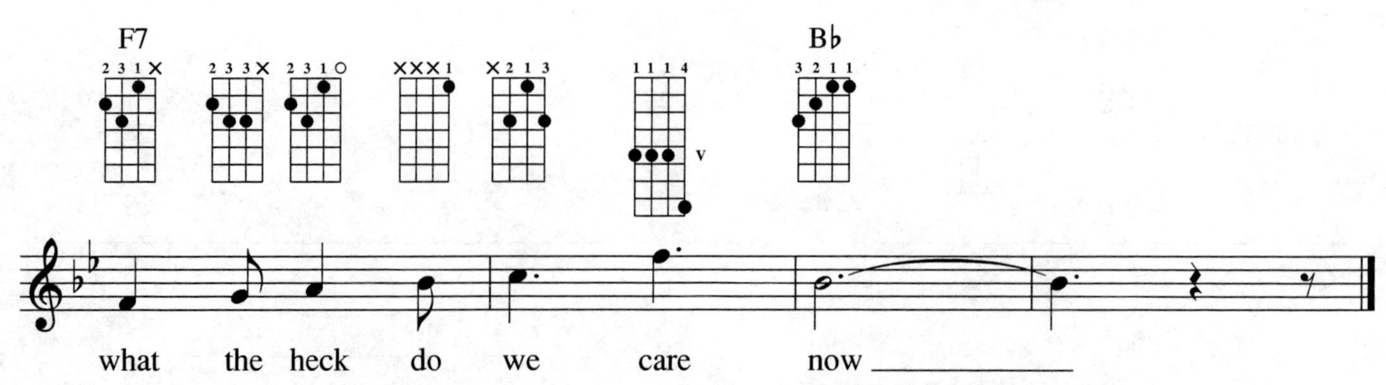

F7
Bb
what the heck do we care now

Chapter 8 - All Chords of the Ukulele

These are all of the chords of the ukulele. Print them out and use them.

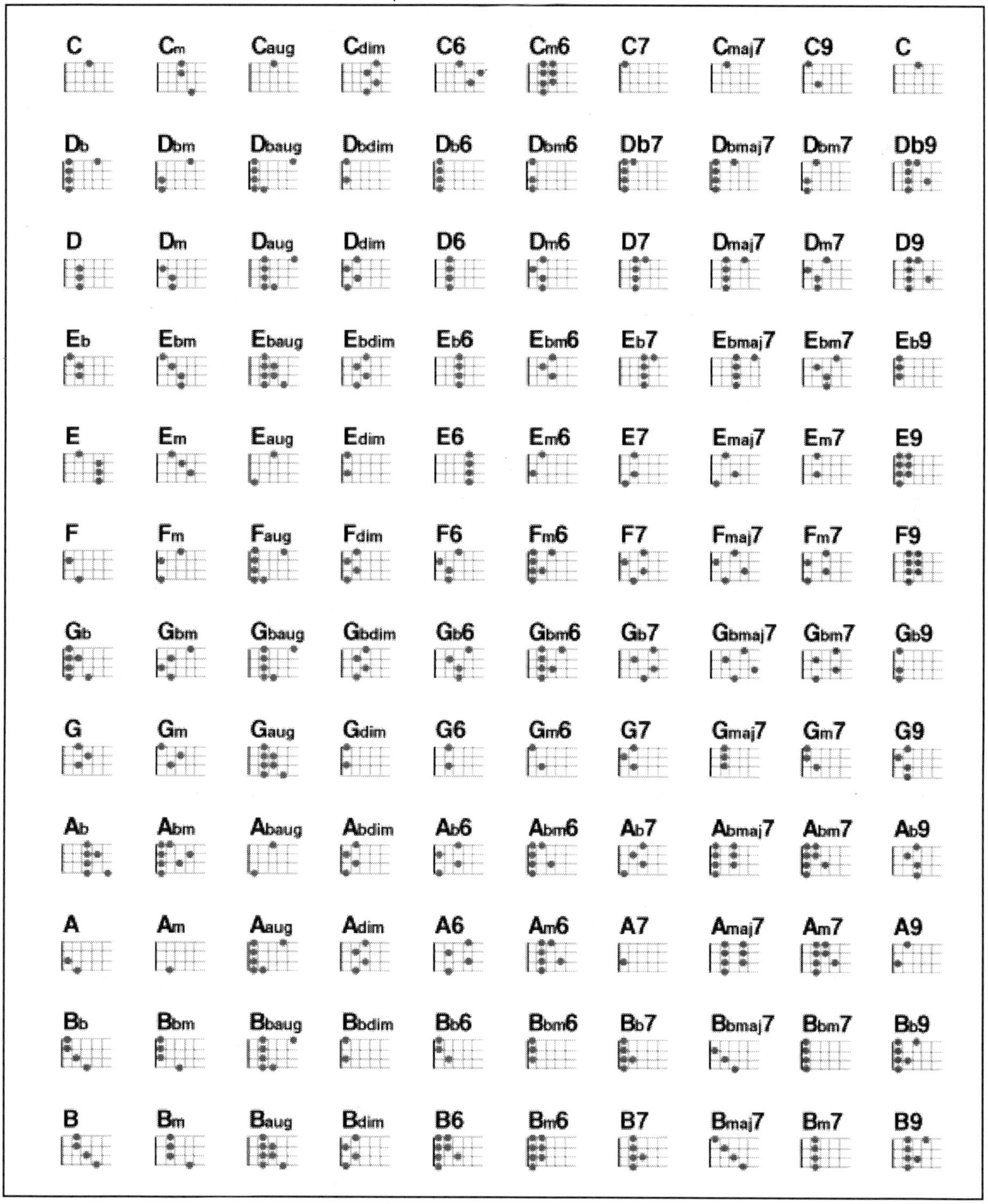

C	Cm	Caug	Cdim	C6	Cm6	C7	Cmaj7	C9	C
Db	Dbm	Dbaug	Dbdim	Db6	Dbm6	Db7	Dbmaj7	Dbm7	Db9
D	Dm	Daug	Ddim	D6	Dm6	D7	Dmaj7	Dm7	D9
Eb	Ebm	Ebaug	Ebdim	Eb6	Ebm6	Eb7	Ebmaj7	Ebm7	Eb9
E	Em	Eaug	Edim	E6	Em6	E7	Emaj7	Em7	E9
F	Fm	Faug	Fdim	F6	Fm6	F7	Fmaj7	Fm7	F9
Gb	Gbm	Gbaug	Gbdim	Gb6	Gbm6	Gb7	Gbmaj7	Gbm7	Gb9
G	Gm	Gaug	Gdim	G6	Gm6	G7	Gmaj7	Gm7	G9
Ab	Abm	Abaug	Abdim	Ab6	Abm6	Ab7	Abmaj7	Abm7	Ab9
A	Am	Aaug	Adim	A6	Am6	A7	Amaj7	Am7	A9
Bb	Bbm	Bbaug	Bbdim	Bb6	Bbm6	Bb7	Bbmaj7	Bbm7	Bb9
B	Bm	Baug	Bdim	B6	Bm6	B7	Bmaj7	Bm7	B9

THE WORLD IS WAITING FOR THE SUNRISE

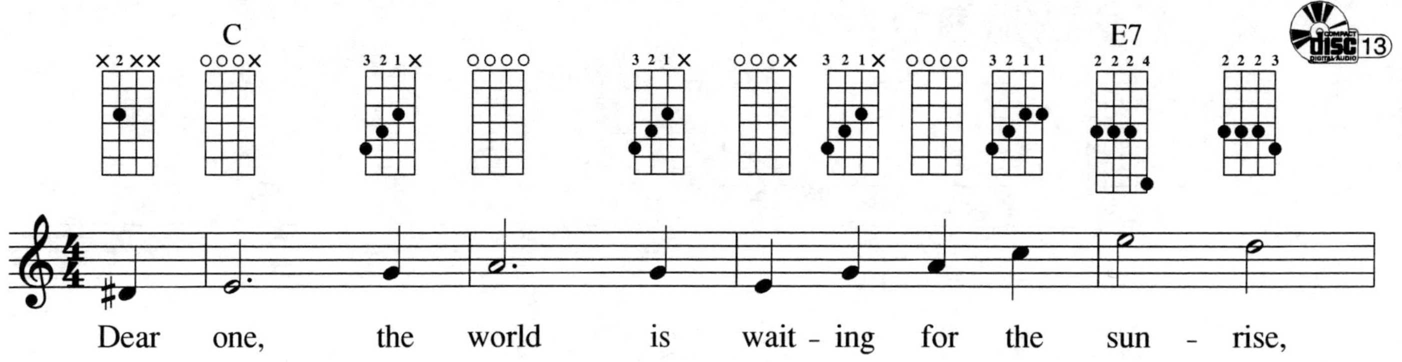
C
E7
Dear one, the world is waiting for the sun - rise,

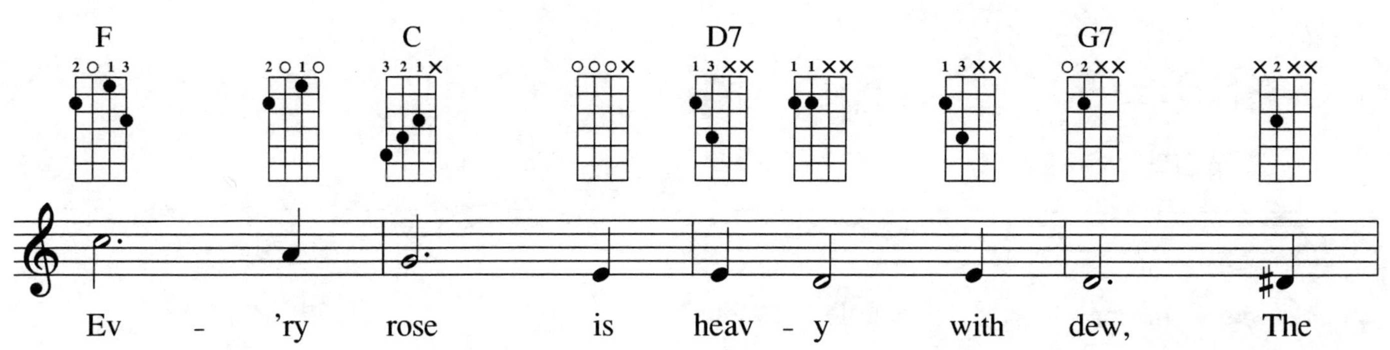
F
C
D7
G7
Ev - 'ry rose is heav - y with dew, The

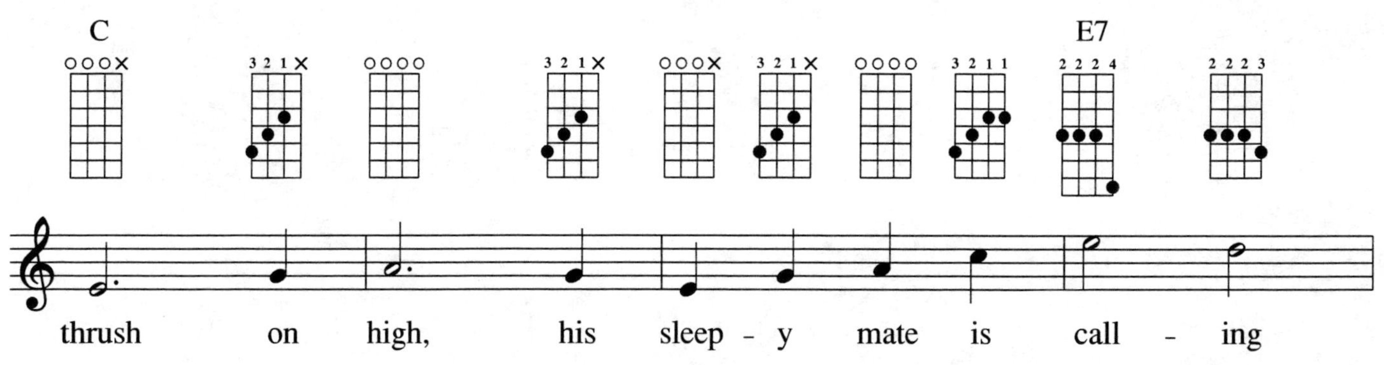
C
E7
thrush on high, his sleep - y mate is call - ing

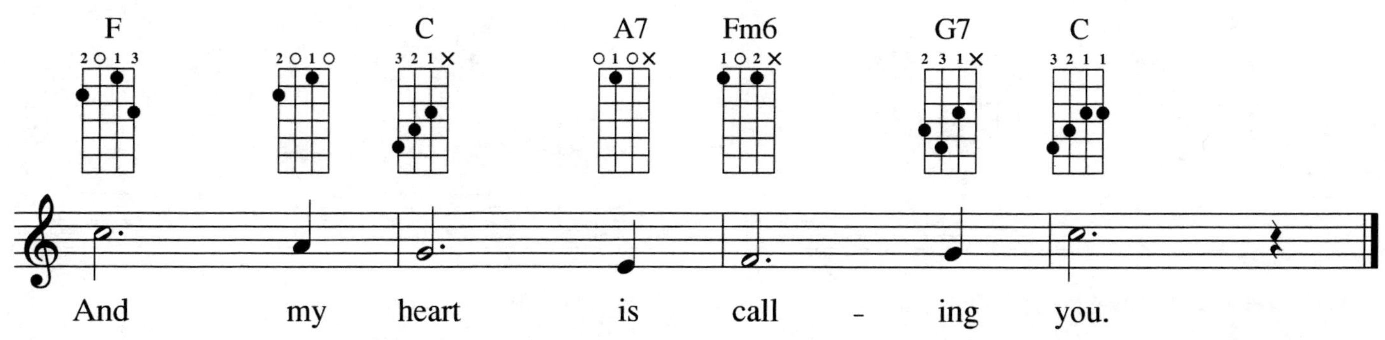
F
C
A7
Fm6
G7
C
And my heart is call - ing you.

14

BILL BAILEY

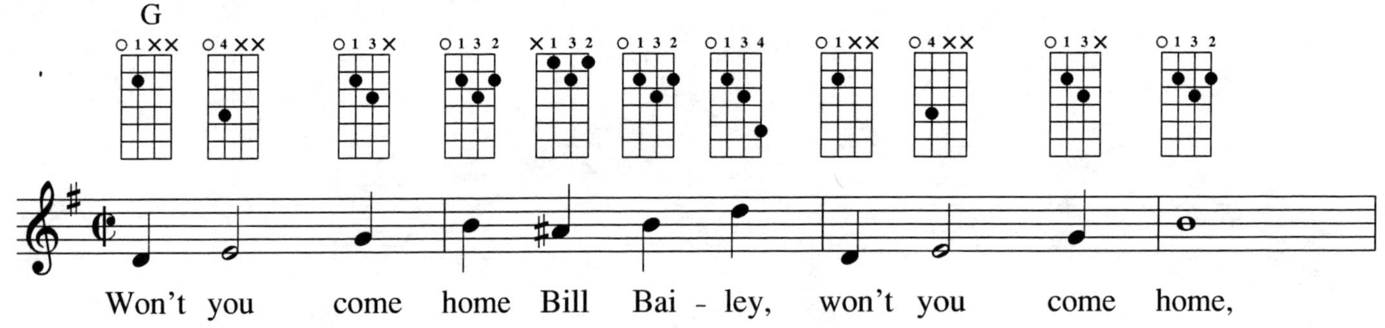
G
Won't you come home Bill Bai - ley, won't you come home,

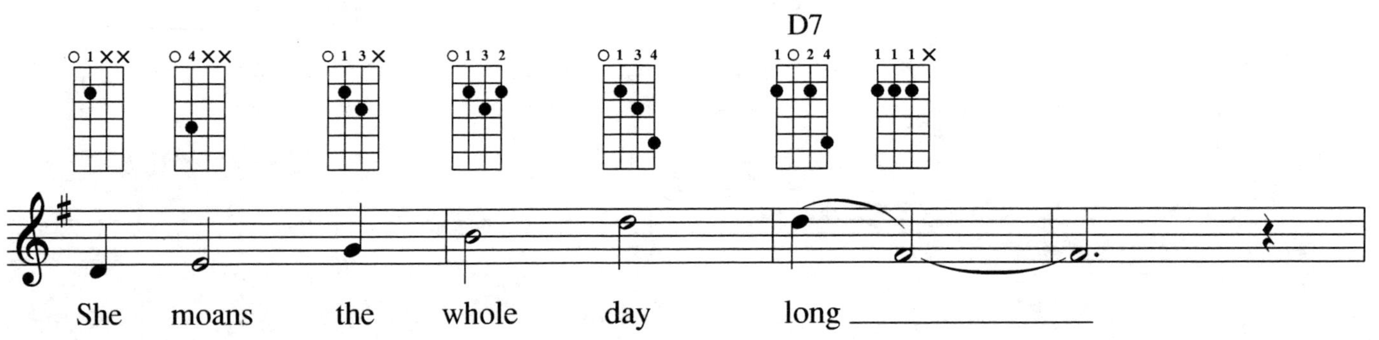
D7
She moans the whole day long

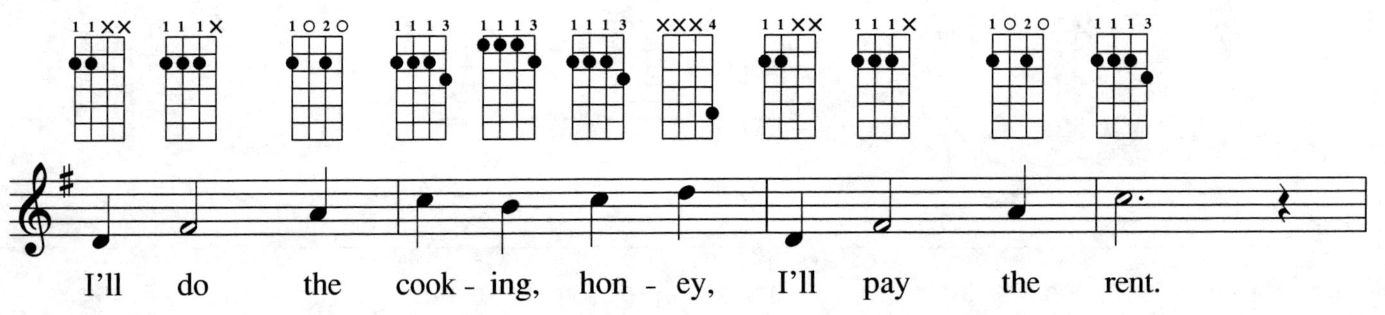
I'll do the cook - ing, hon - ey, I'll pay the rent.

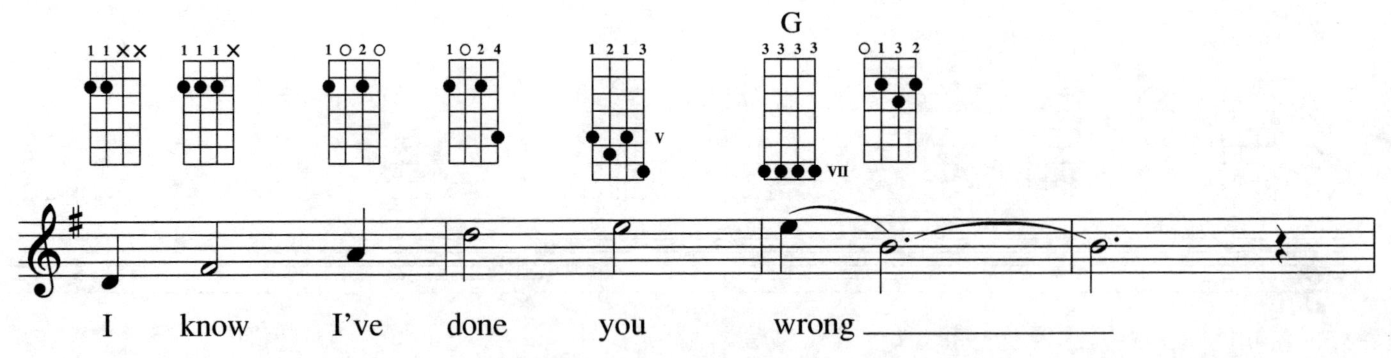
G
I know I've done you wrong

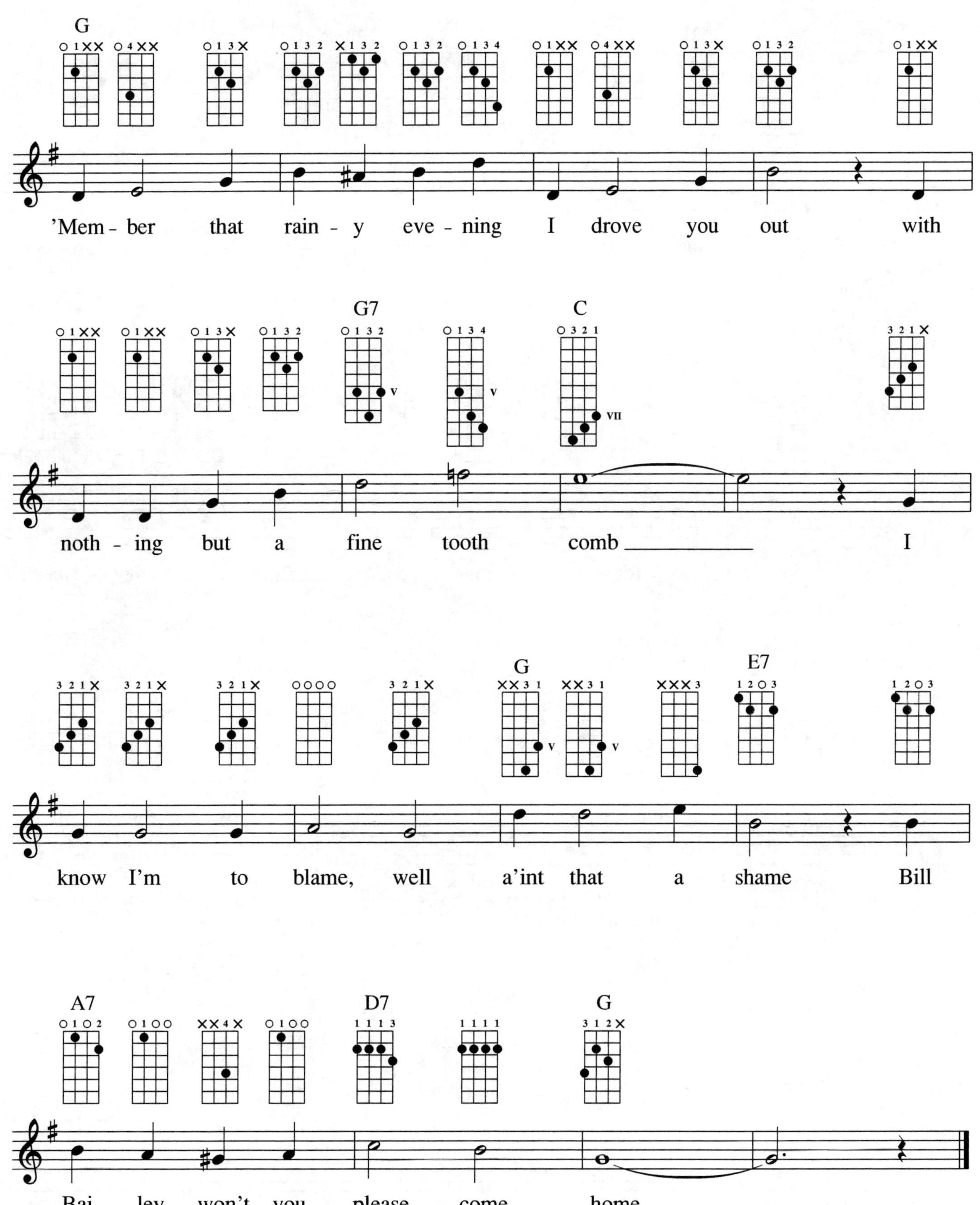
G
'Mem - ber that rain - y eve - ning I drove you out with
G7
C
noth - ing but a fine tooth comb I
G
E7
know I'm to blame, well a'int that a shame Bill
A7
D7
G
Bai - ley won't you please come home

COMPACT
DISC
DIGITAL AUDIO
15

FOR ME AND MY GAL

D7
G
The bells are ring - ing ____ for me and my gal ____ The birds are

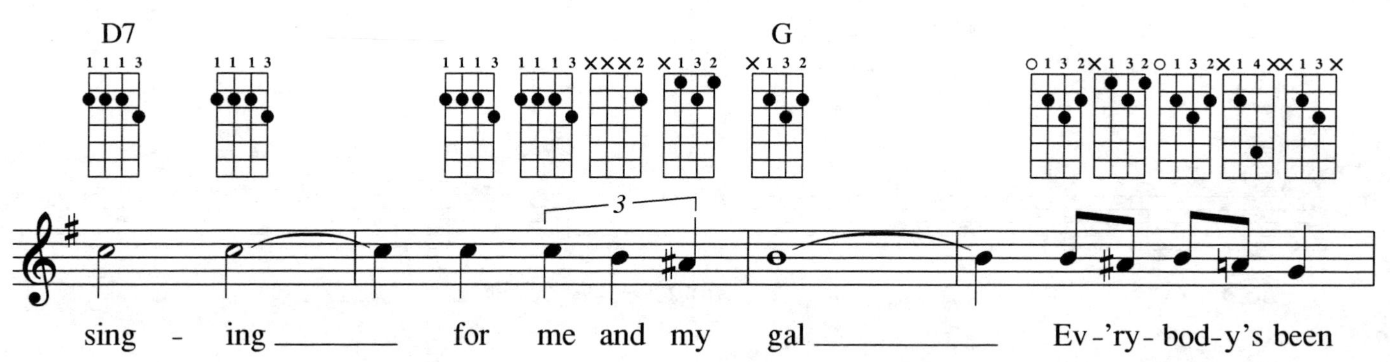
D7
G
sing - ing ____ for me and my gal ____ Ev - 'ry - bod - y's been

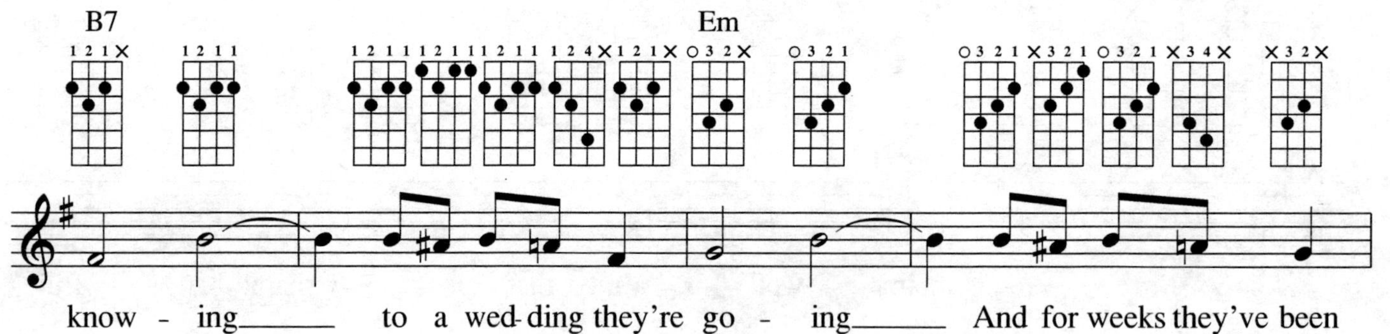
B7
Em
know - ing ____ to a wed-ding they're go - ing ____ And for weeks they've been

A7
D7
Bdim7
D7
sew - ing ____ ev - 'ry Su - sie and Sal ____ They're con - gre -

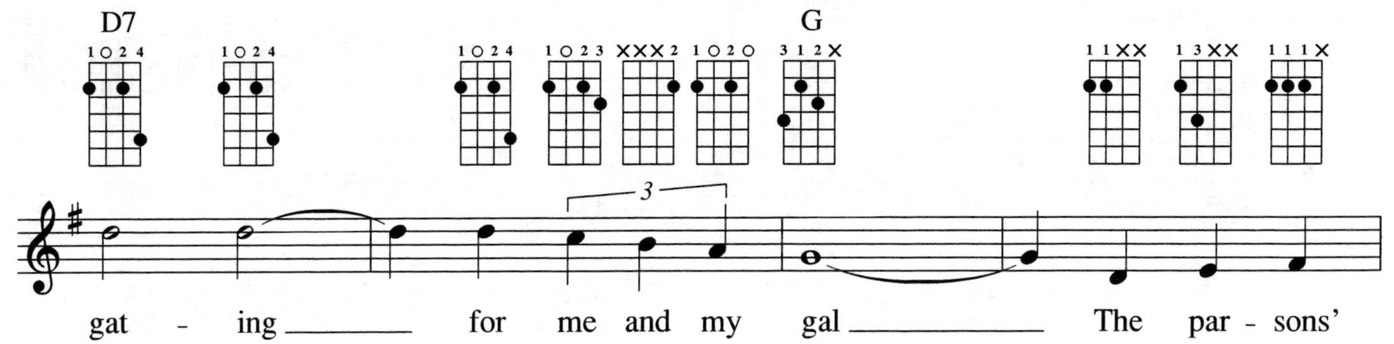
D7
G
gat - ing for me and my gal The par - sons'

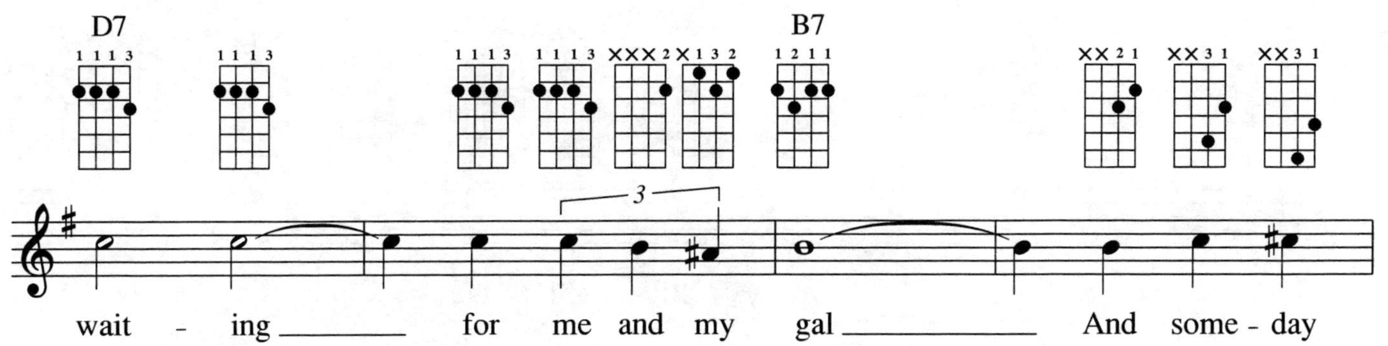
D7
B7
wait - ing for me and my gal And some - day

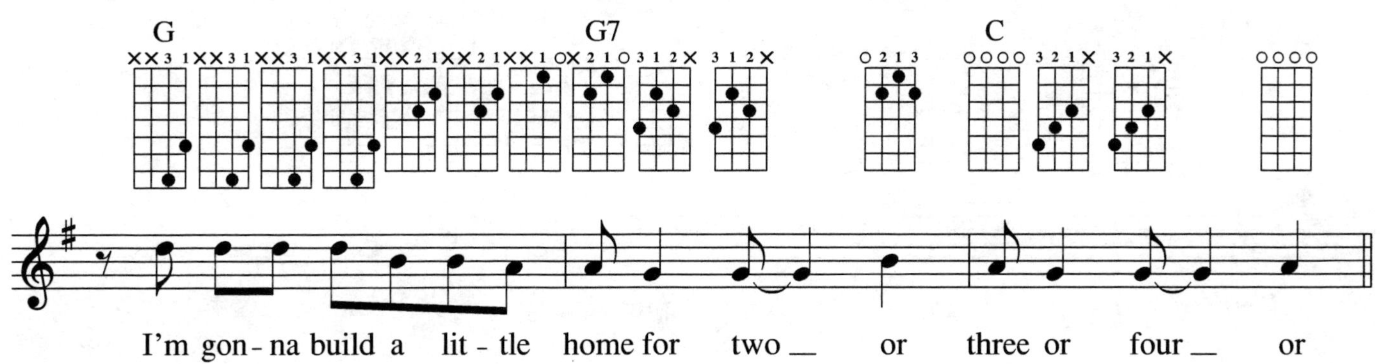
G
G7
C
I'm gon - na build a lit - tle home for two or three or four or

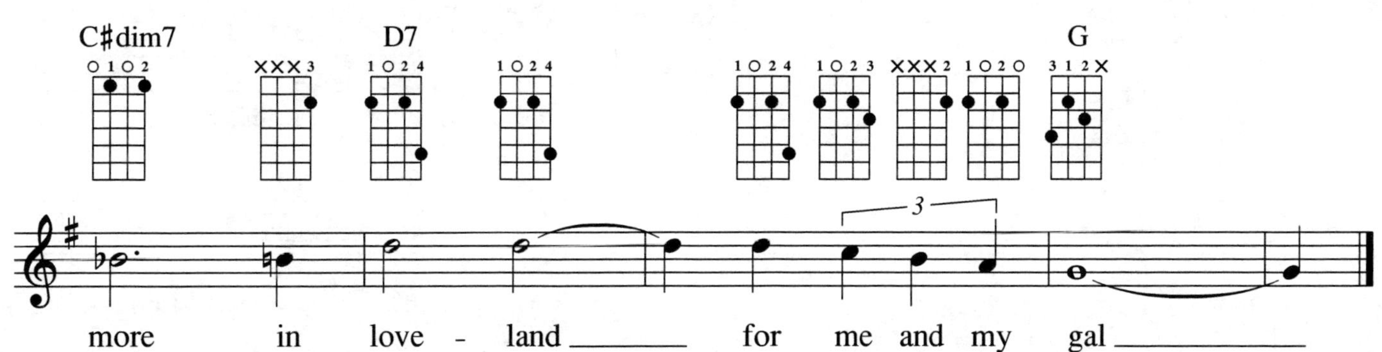
C♯dim7
D7
G
more in love - land for me and my gal

COMPACT
disc
DIGITAL AUDIO
16

MARGIE

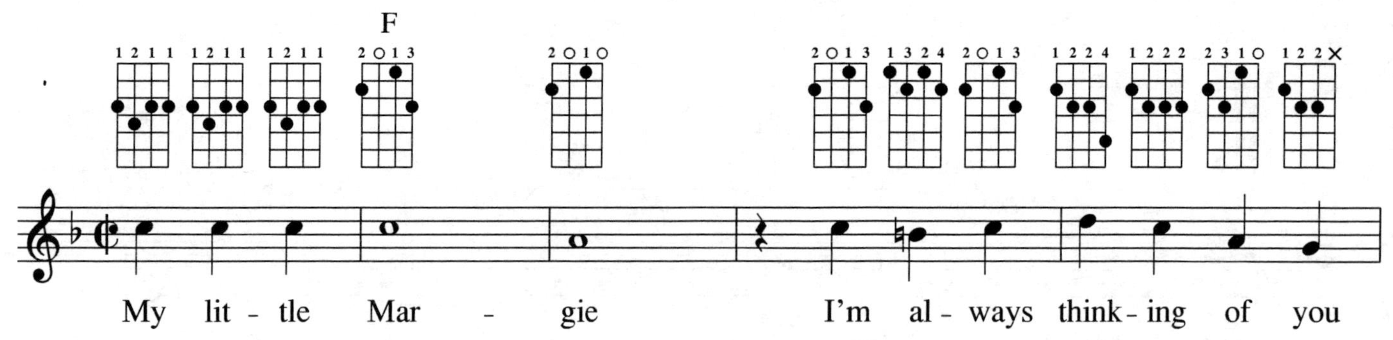

F
My lit - tle Mar - gie
I'm al - ways think - ing of you

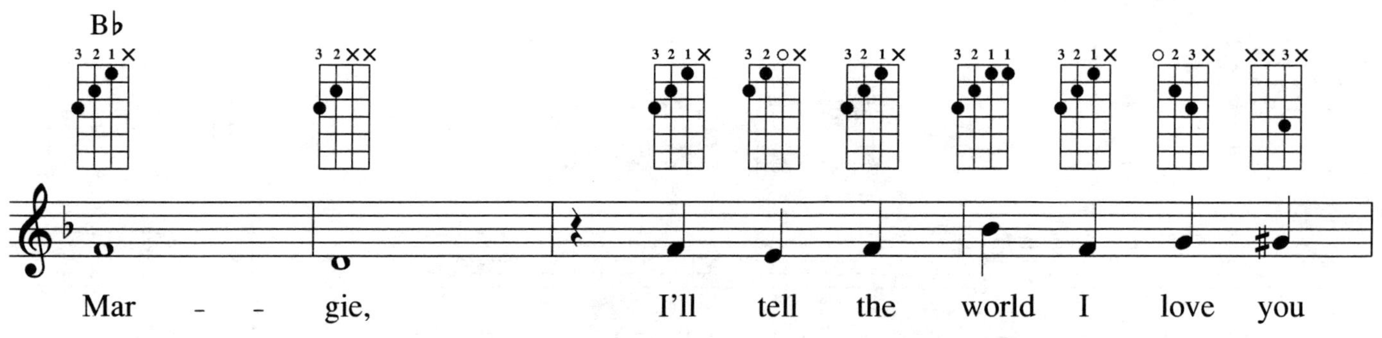

B♭
Mar - - gie,
I'll tell the world I love you

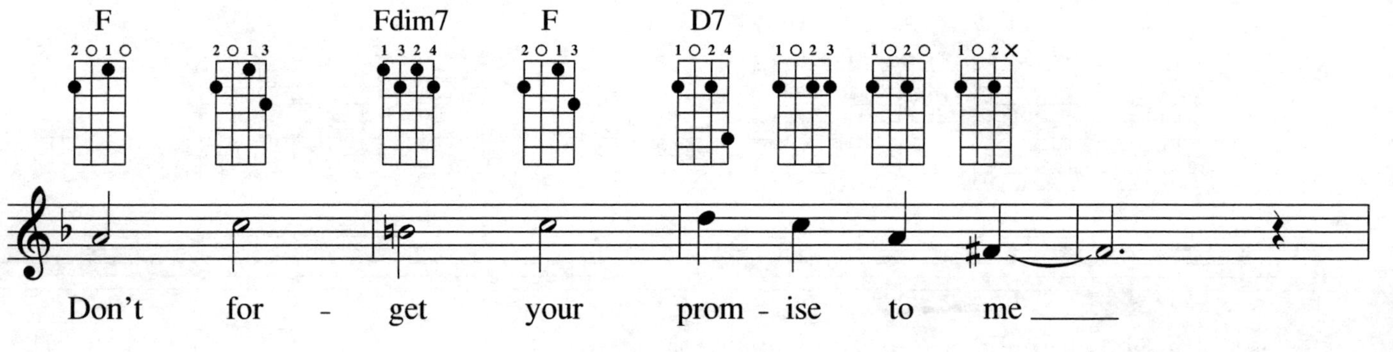

F
Fdim7
F
D7
Don't for - get your prom - ise to me ____

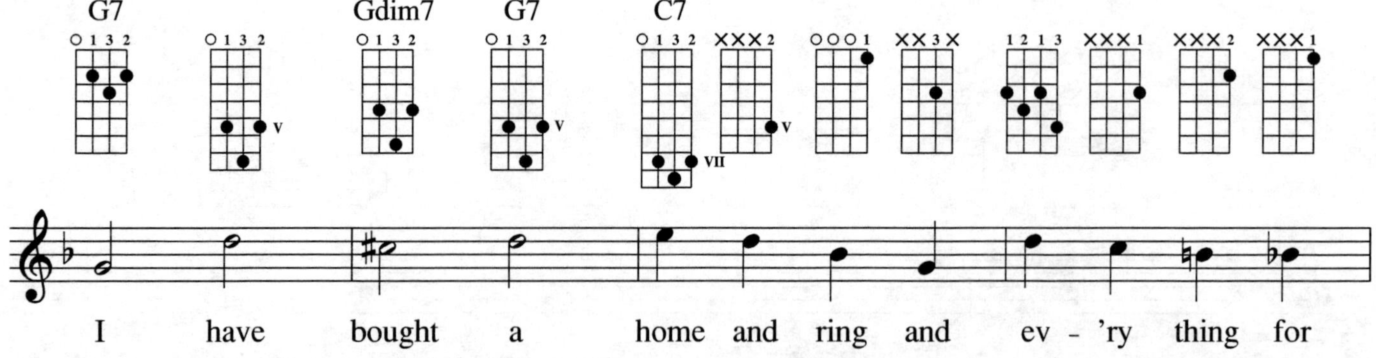

G7
Gdim7
G7
C7
I have bought a home and ring and ev - 'ry thing for

F
2 0 1 3
2 0 1 0
2 0 1 3
1 3 2 1
2 0 1 3
1 2 2 4
1 2 2 2
2 3 1 0
1 2 2
Mar - - gie You've been my in - spi - ra - tion

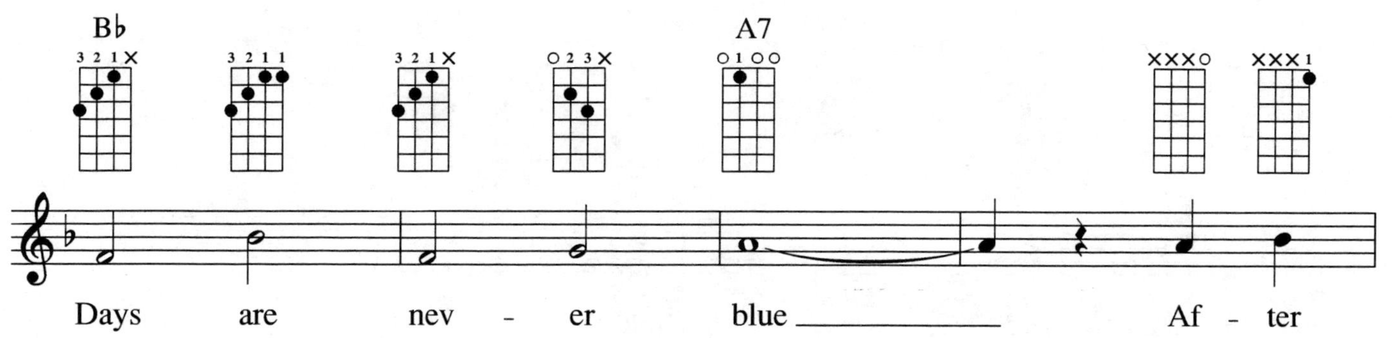
B♭
3 2 1
3 2 1 1
3 2 1
0 2 3
A7
0 1 0 0
0
1
Days are nev - er blue After

F
2 0 1 3
4
2 0 1 3
4
2 0 1 3
2 0 1 0
1
2 0 1 3
4
2 0 1 3
4
D7
1 2 1 3
1 2 1 1
all is said and done, There is real - ly on - ly one, Oh

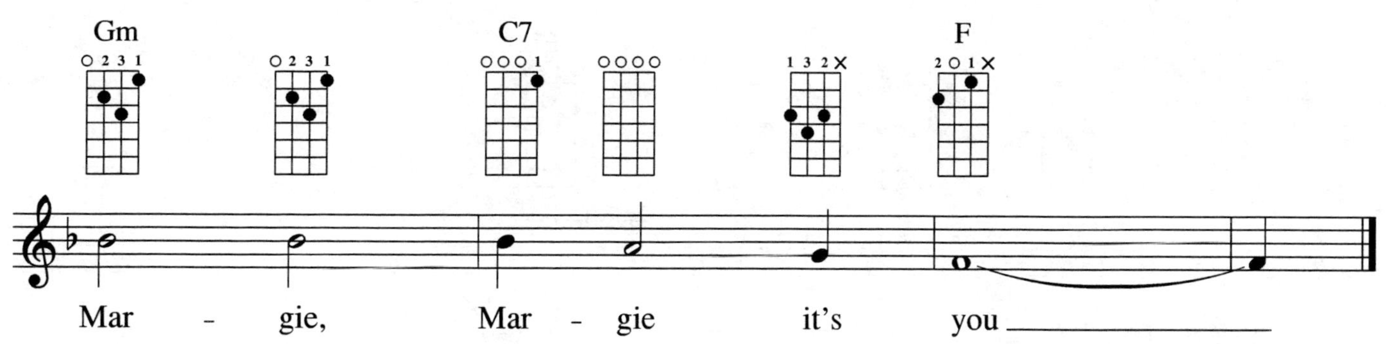
Gm
0 2 3 1
0 2 3 1
C7
0 0 0 1
0 0 0 0
1 3 2
F
2 0 1
Mar - gie, Mar - gie it's you

disc
17

I WANT A GIRL

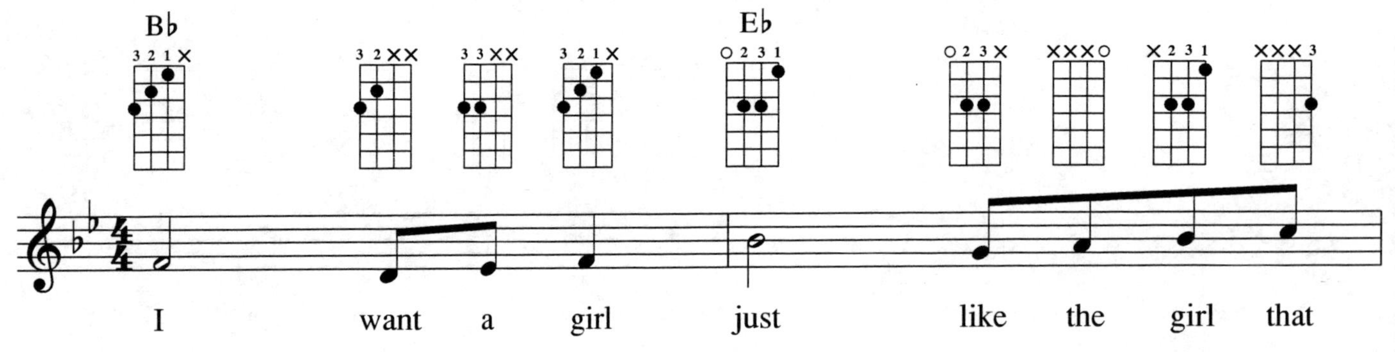
B♭
E♭
I want a girl just like the girl that

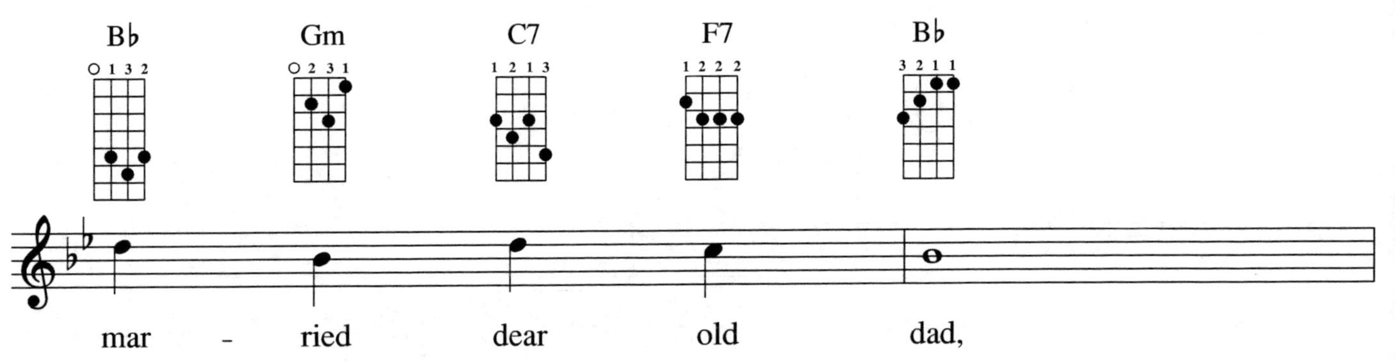
B♭
Gm
C7
F7
B♭
mar - ried dear old dad,

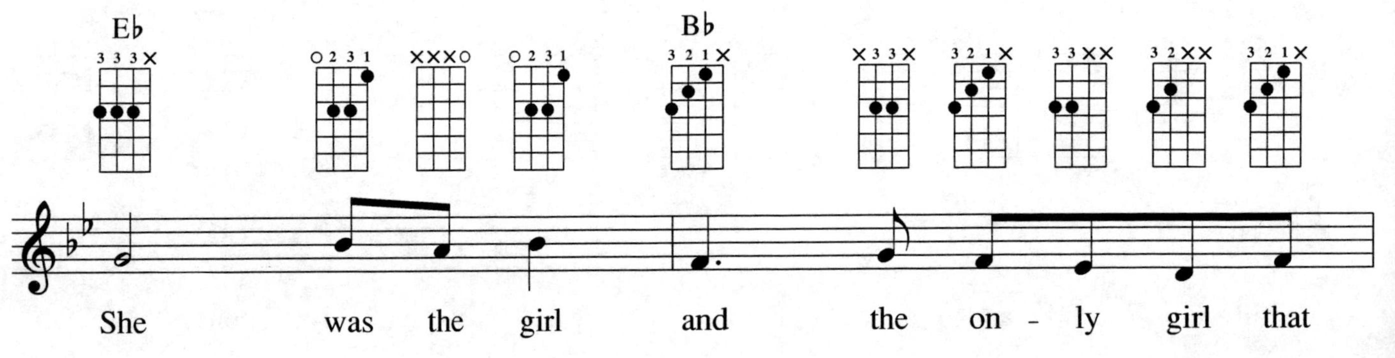
E♭
B♭
She was the girl and the on - ly girl that

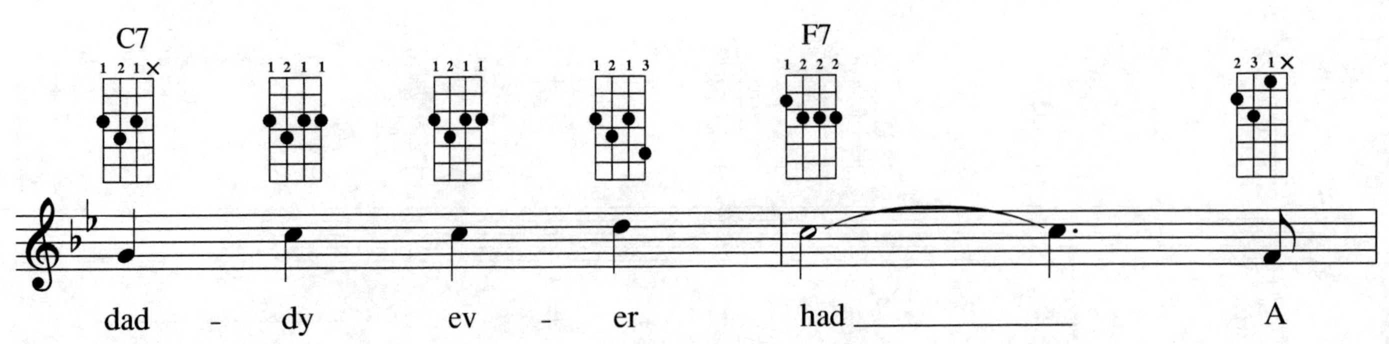
C7
F7
dad - dy ev - er had
A

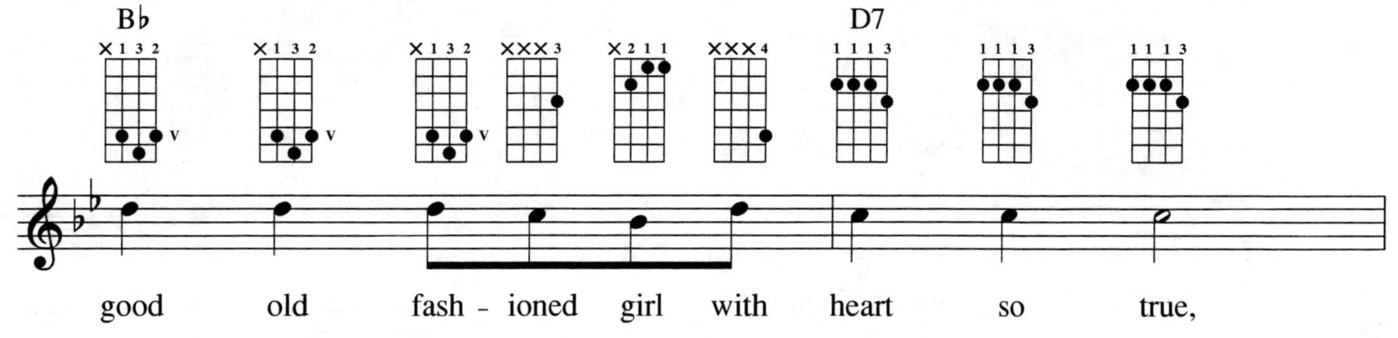
B♭
D7
good old fash - ioned girl with heart so true,

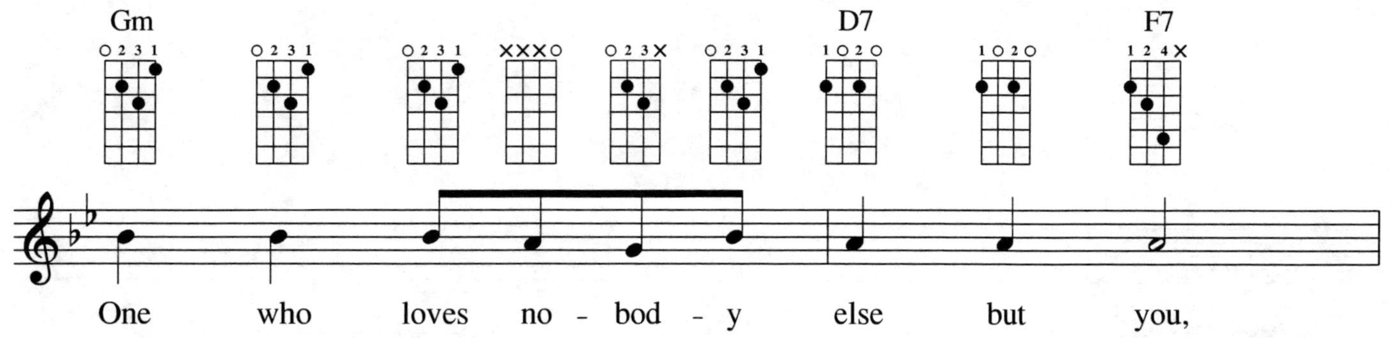
Gm
D7
F7
One who loves no - bod - y else but you,

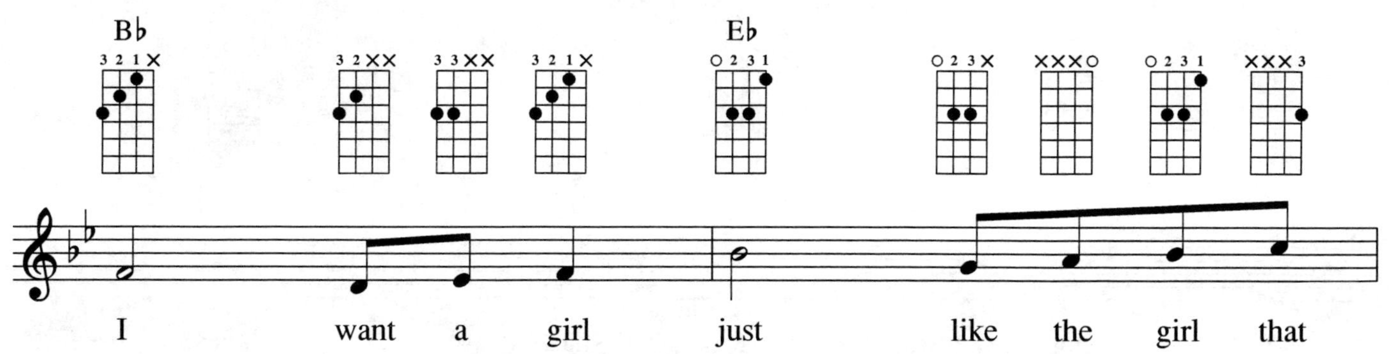
B♭
E♭
I want a girl just like the girl that

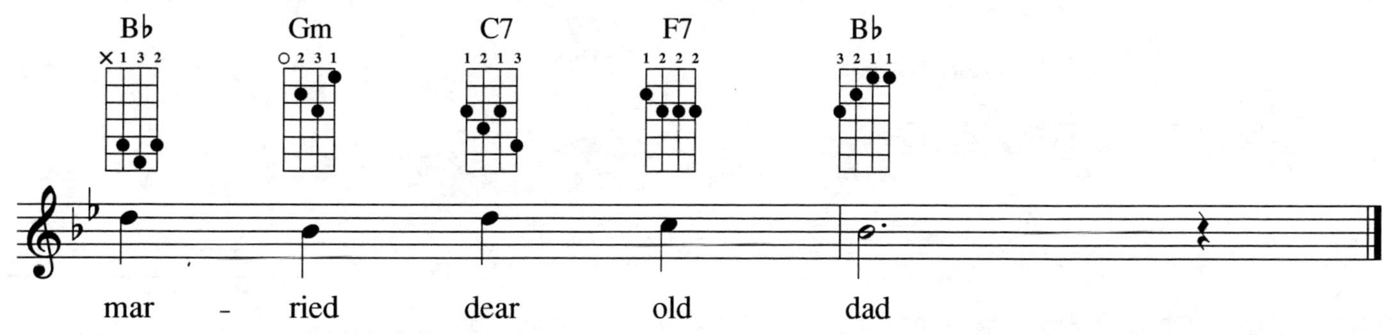
B♭
Gm
C7
F7
B♭
mar - ried dear old dad

IN THE GOOD OLD SUMMER TIME

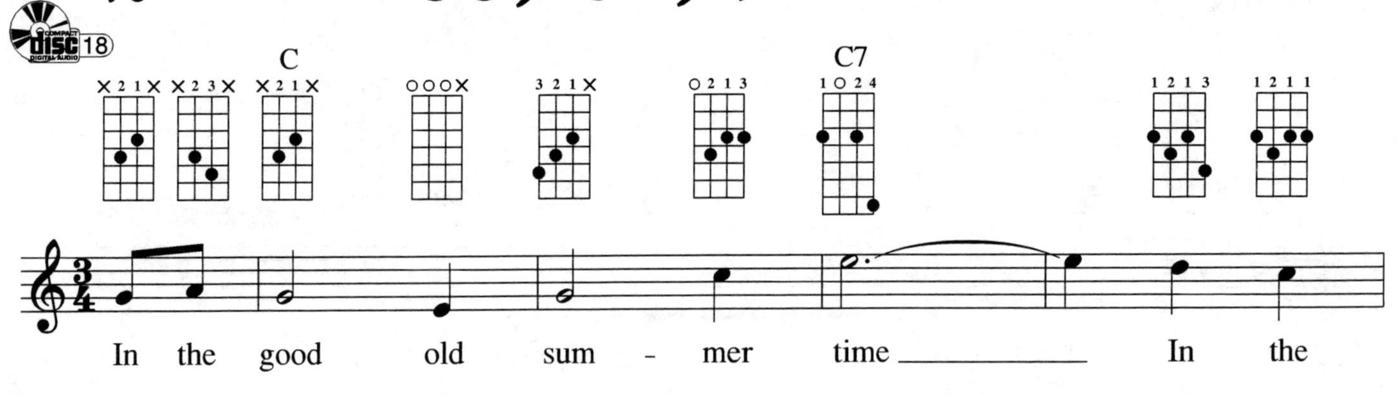
18
C
C7
In the good old sum - mer time ___ In the

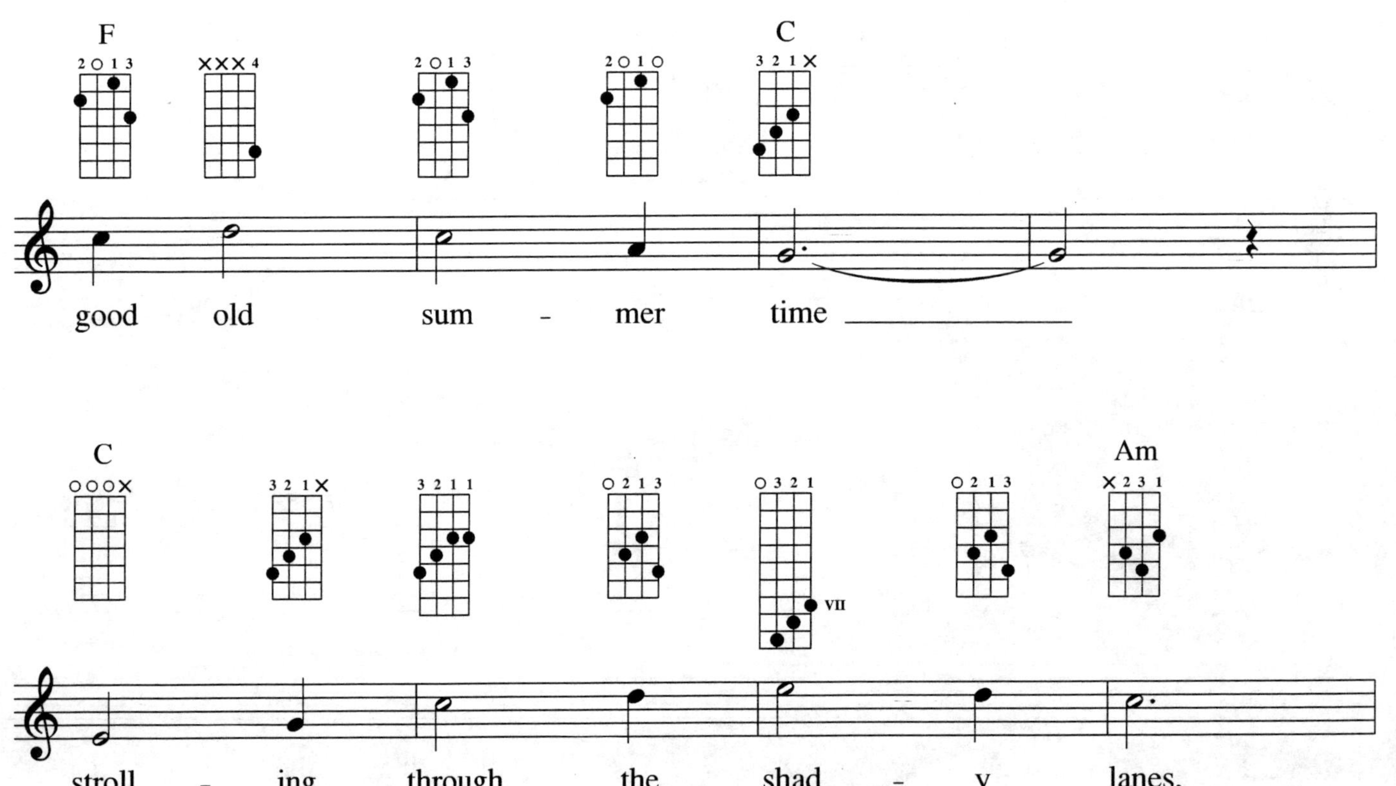
F
C
good old sum - mer time ___
C
Am
VII
stroll - ing through the shad - y lanes,

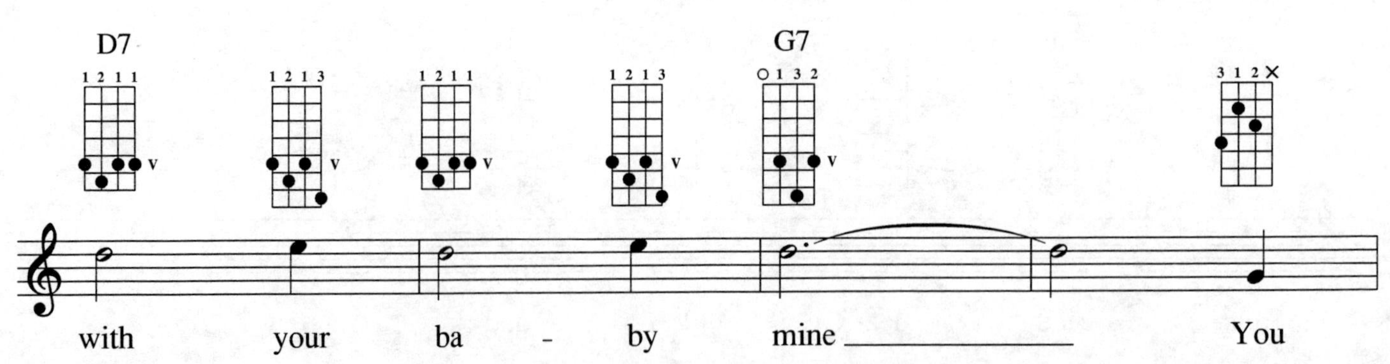
D7
G7
V
with your ba - by mine ___ You

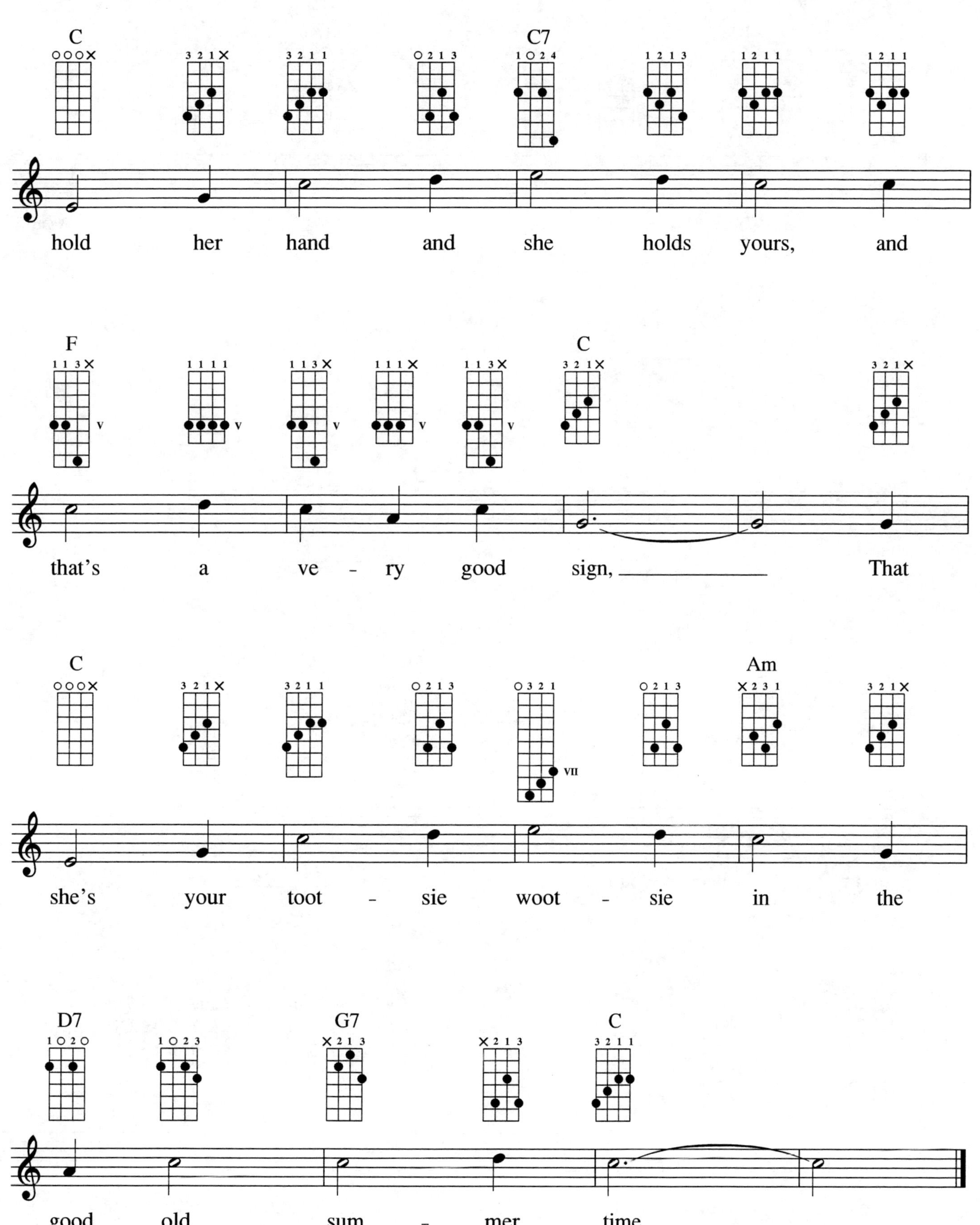
C
C7
hold her hand and she holds yours, and
F
C
that's a ve - ry good sign, ___ That
C
Am
she's your toot - sie woot - sie in the
D7
G7
C
good old sum - mer time ___

disc 19

THE SHEIK OF ARABY

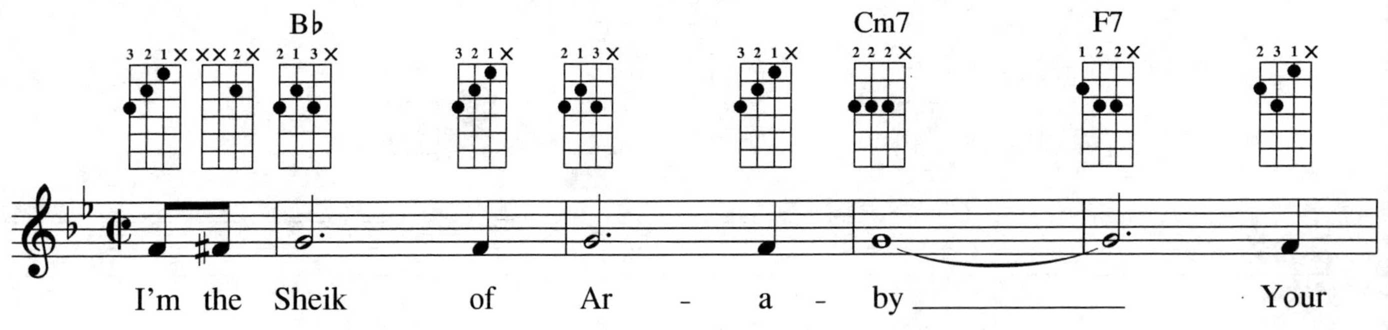
B♭
Cm7
F7
I'm the Sheik of Ar - a - by Your

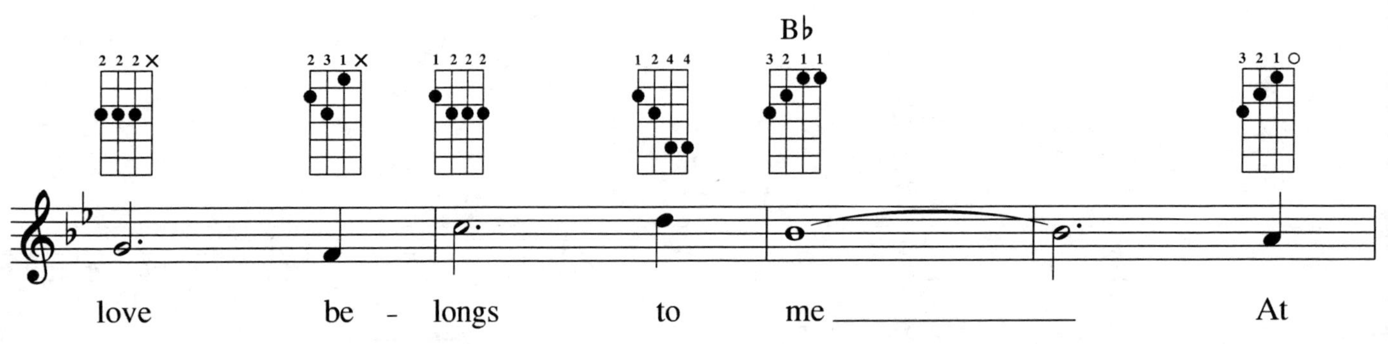
B♭
love be - longs to me At

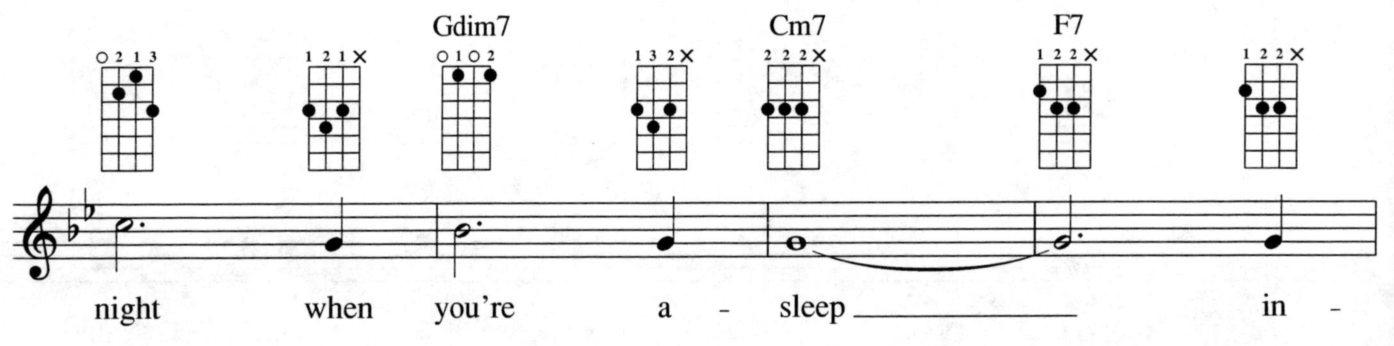
Gdim7
Cm7
F7
night when you're a - sleep in -

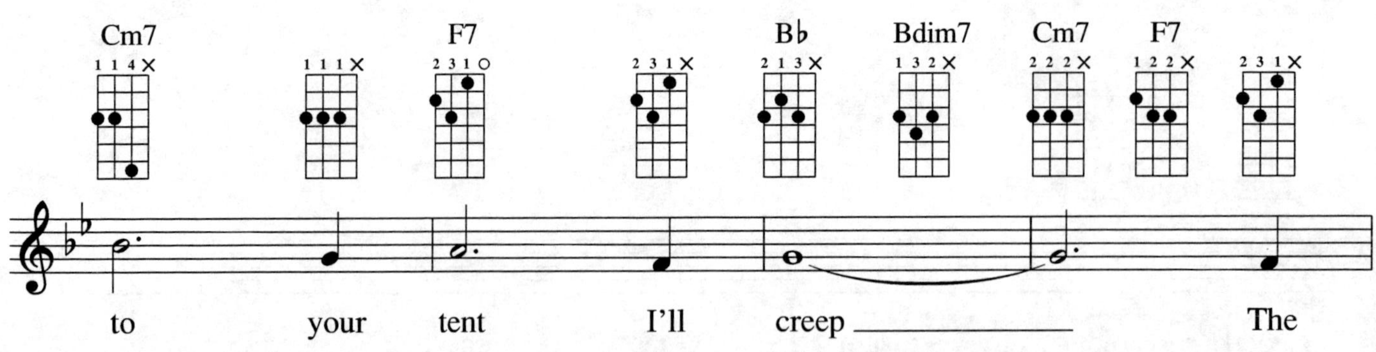
Cm7
F7
B♭
Bdim7
Cm7
F7
to your tent I'll creep The

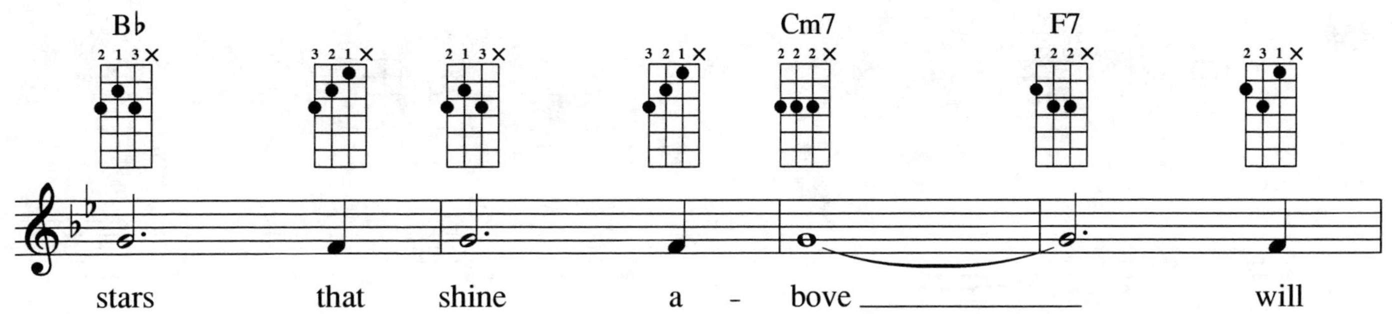
B♭
Cm7
F7
stars that shine a - bove _______ will

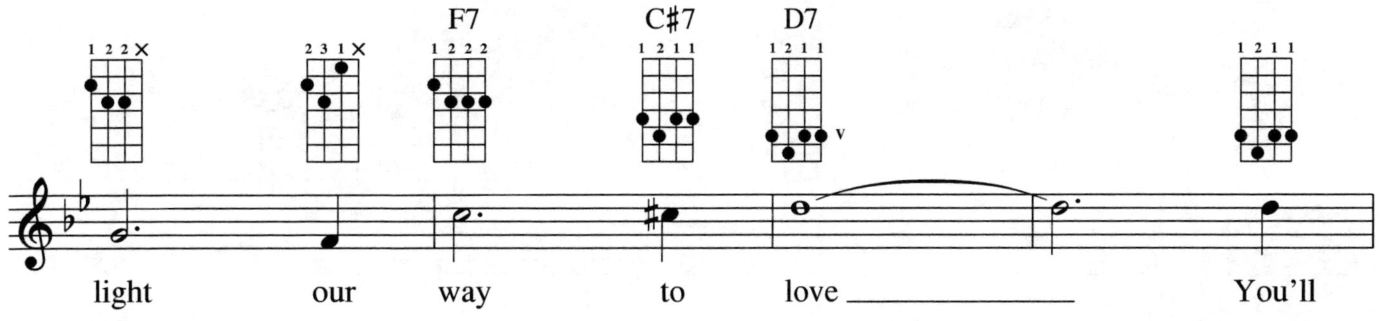
F7
C♯7
D7
light our way to love _______ You'll

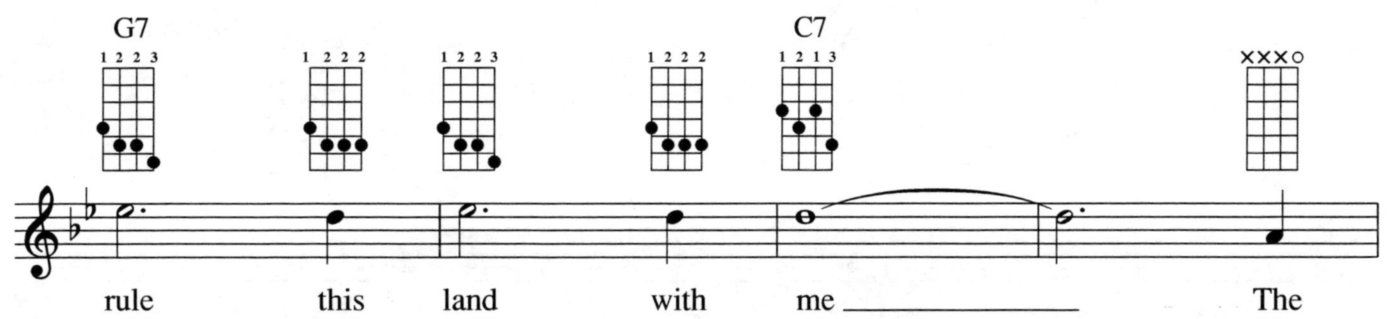
G7
C7
rule this land with me _______ The

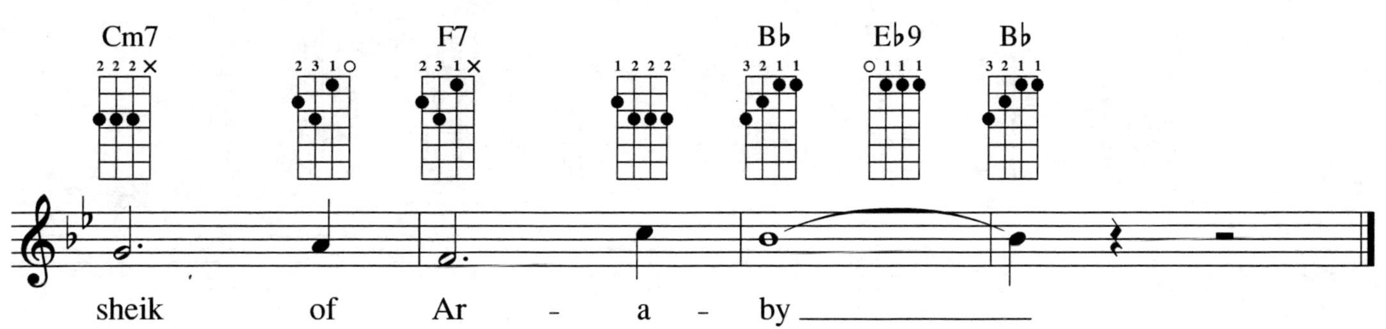
Cm7
F7
B♭
E♭9
B♭
sheik of Ar - a - by _______

BY THE LIGHT OF THE SILVERY MOON

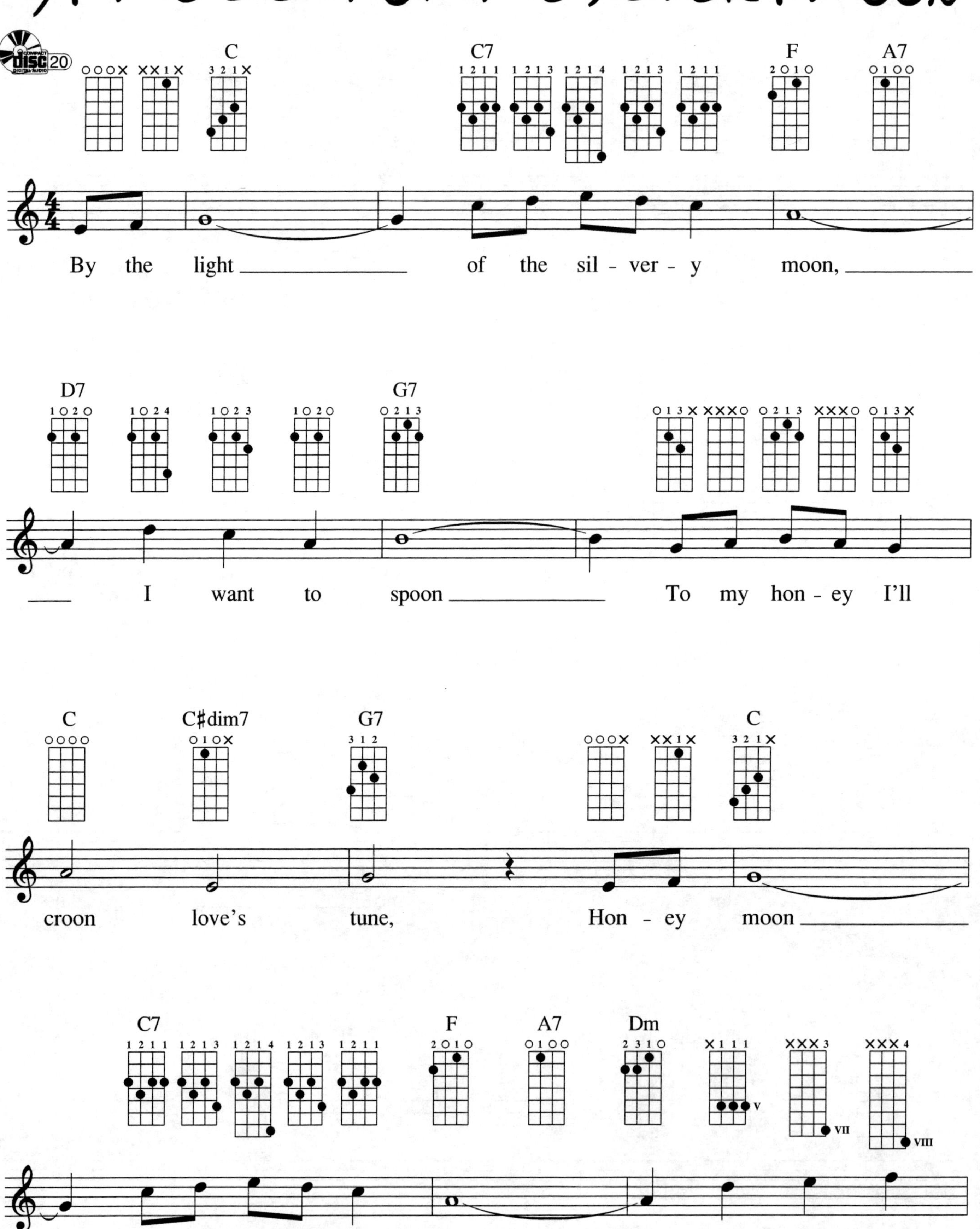
20
C
C7
F
A7
By the light of the sil - ver - y moon,
D7
G7
I want to spoon To my hon - ey I'll
C
C#dim7
G7
C
croon love's tune, Hon - ey moon
C7
F
A7
Dm
Keep a shin - ing in June Your sil - v'ry

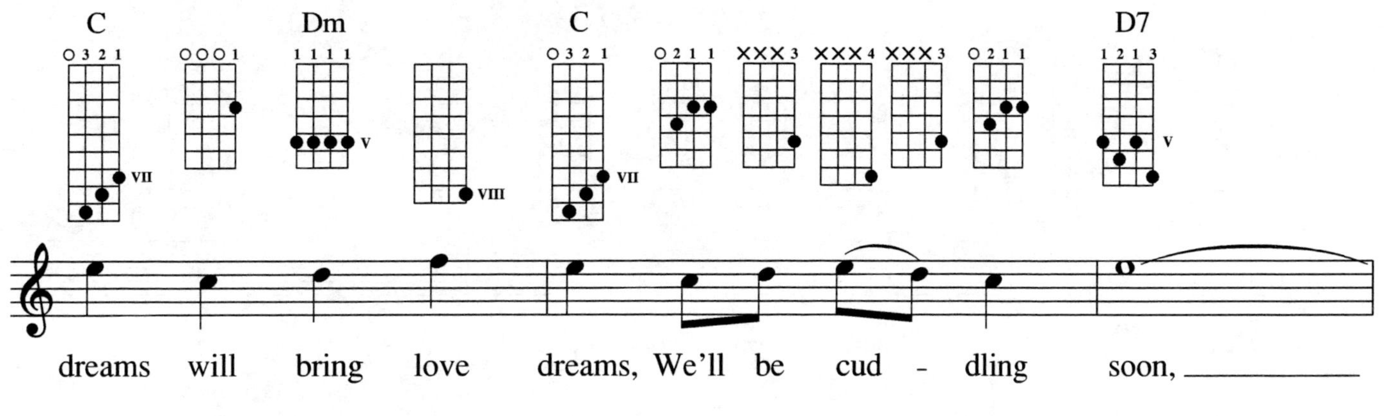
C
Dm
C
D7
dreams will bring love dreams, We'll be cud - dling soon,

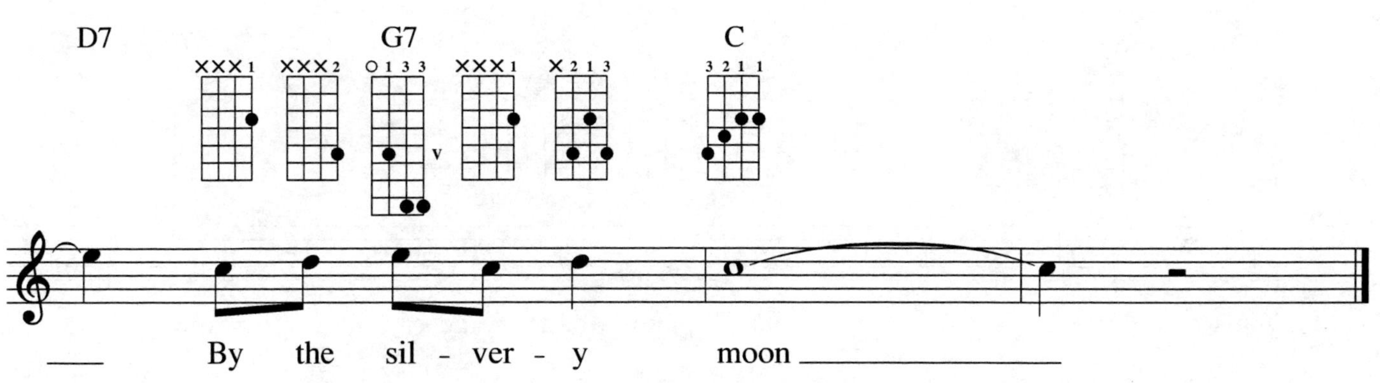
D7
G7
C
By the sil - ver - y moon

disc
21

WHISPERING

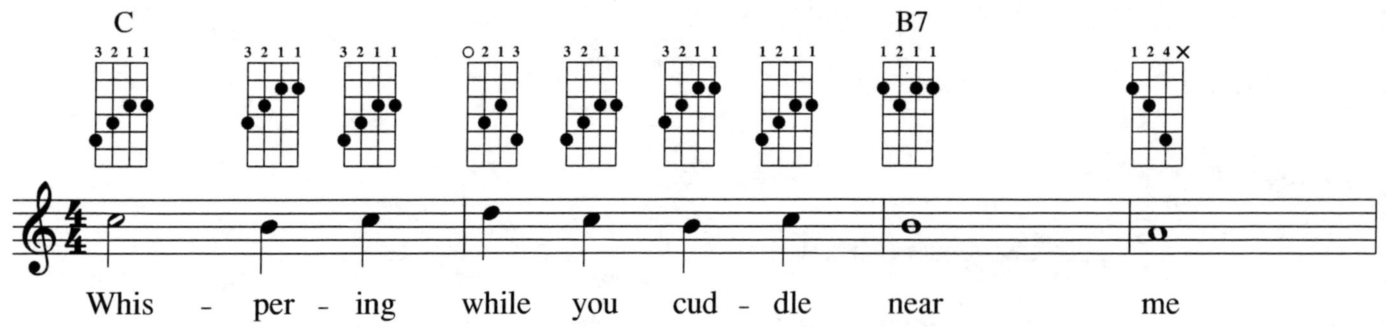
C
B7
Whis - per - ing while you cud - dle near me

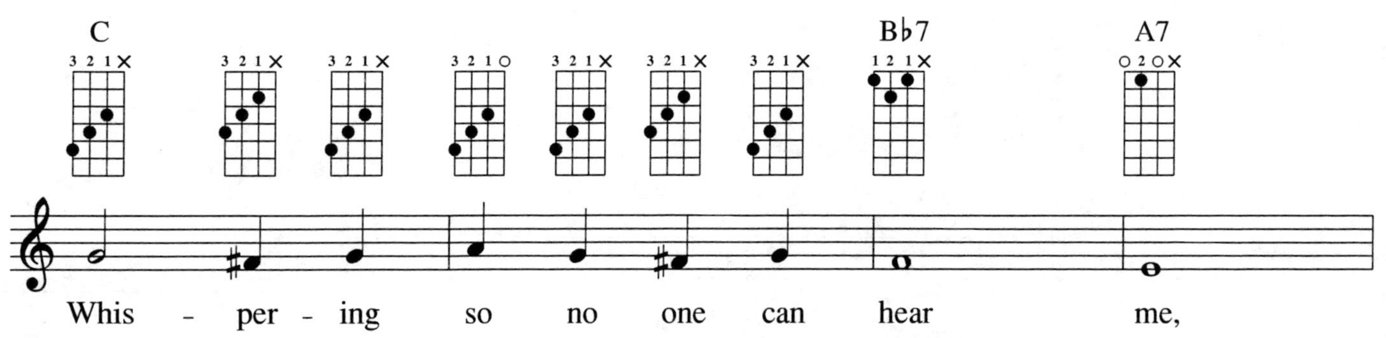
C
B♭7
A7
Whis - per - ing so no one can hear me,

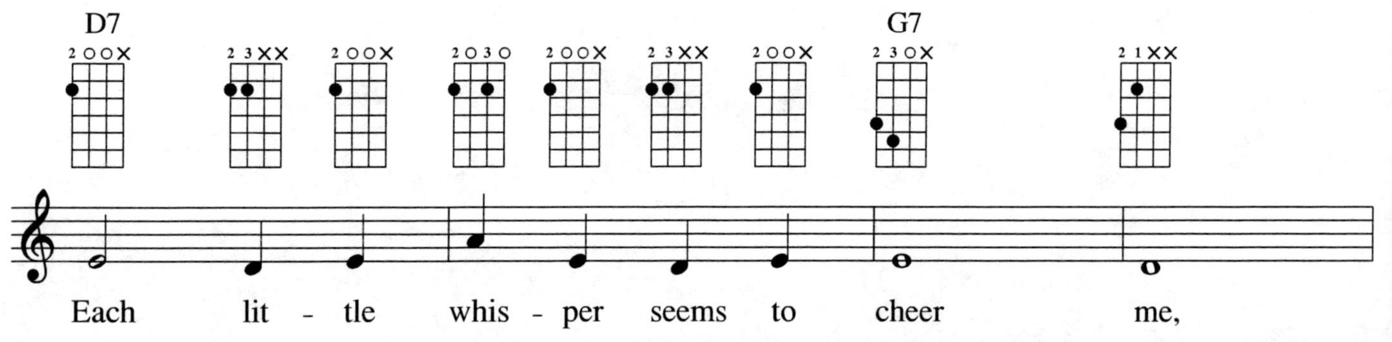
D7
G7
Each lit - tle whis - per seems to cheer me,

C
Am
Dm
G7
I know it's true there's no one dear but you, You're

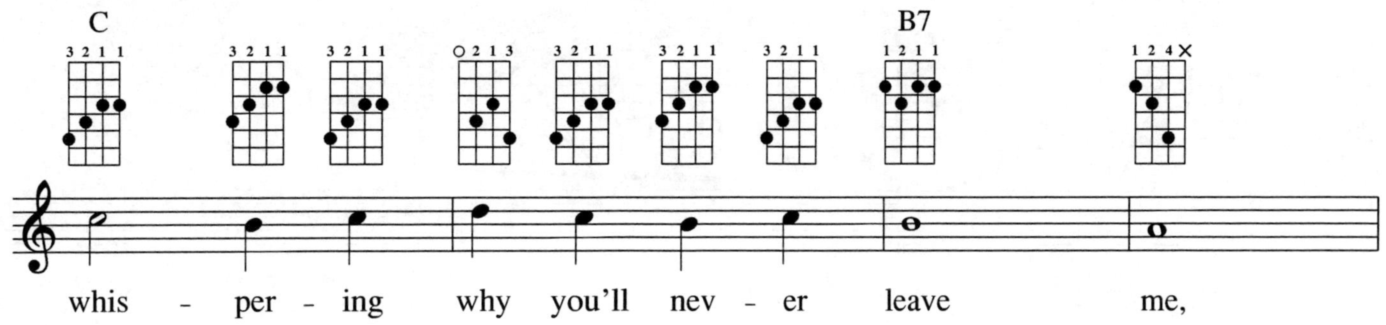
C
B7
whis - per - ing why you'll nev - er leave me,

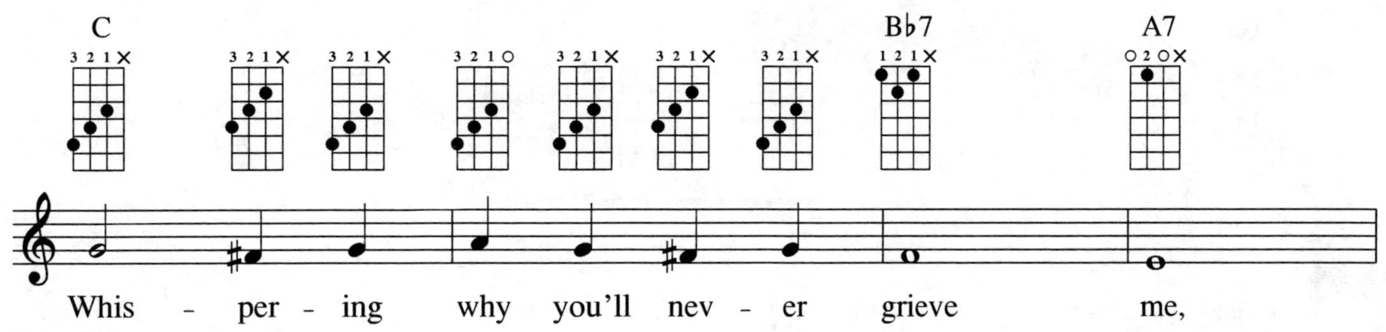
C
B♭7
A7
Whis - per - ing why you'll nev - er grieve me,

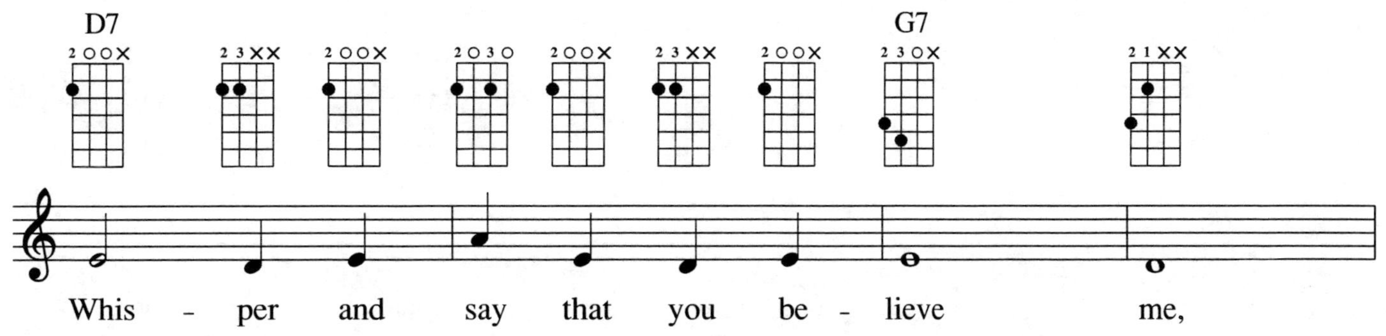
D7
G7
Whis - per and say that you be - lieve me,

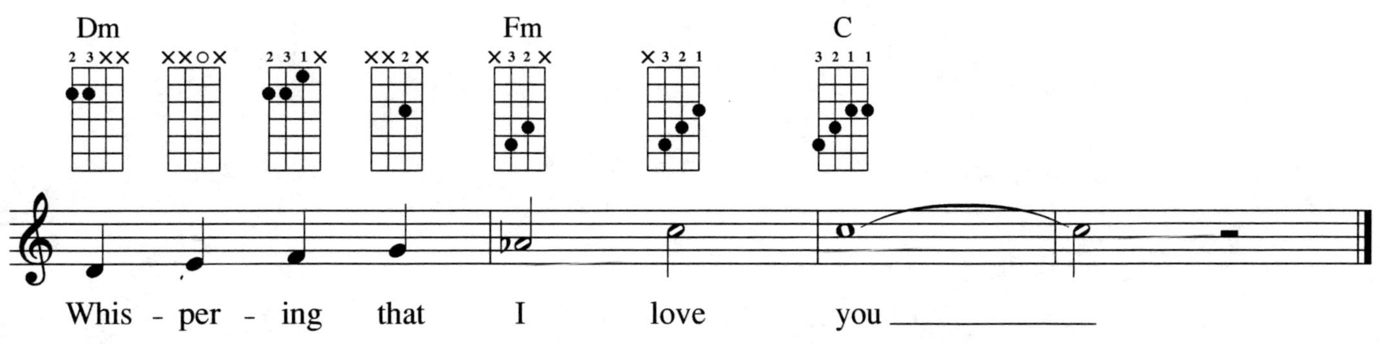
Dm
Fm
C
Whis - per - ing that I love you

OH, YOU BEAUTIFUL DOLL

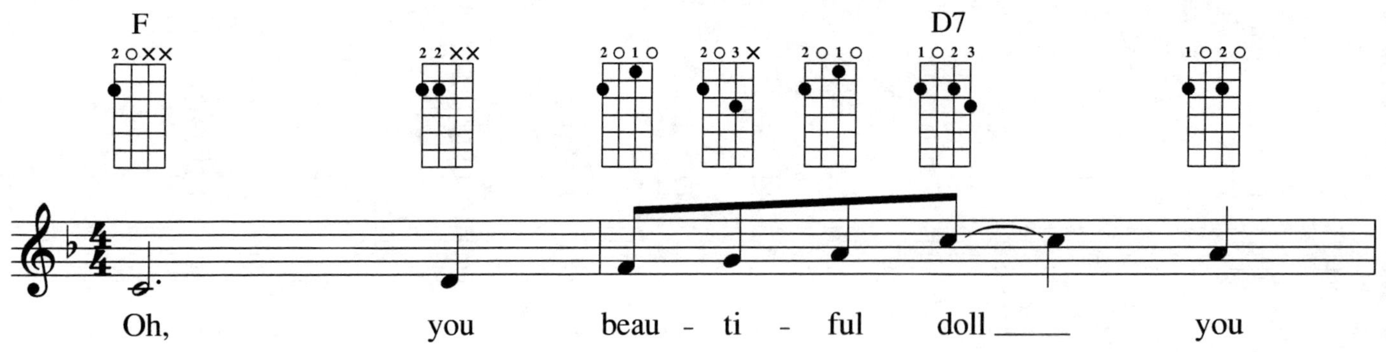
F
D7
Oh, you beau - ti - ful doll you

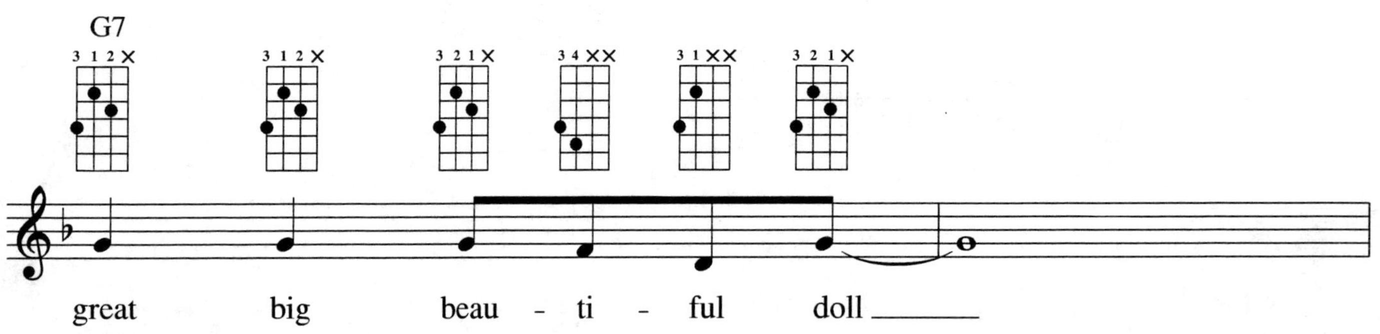
G7
great big beau - ti - ful doll

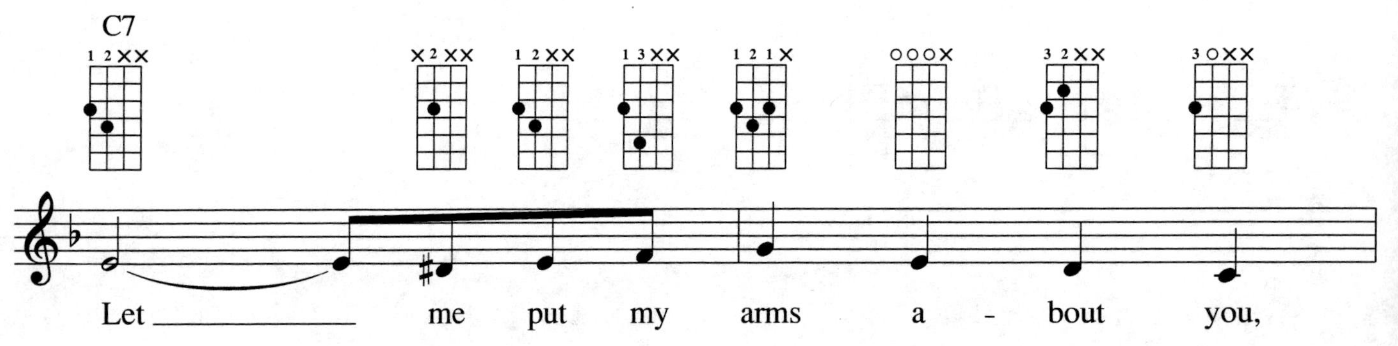
C7
Let me put my arms a - bout you,

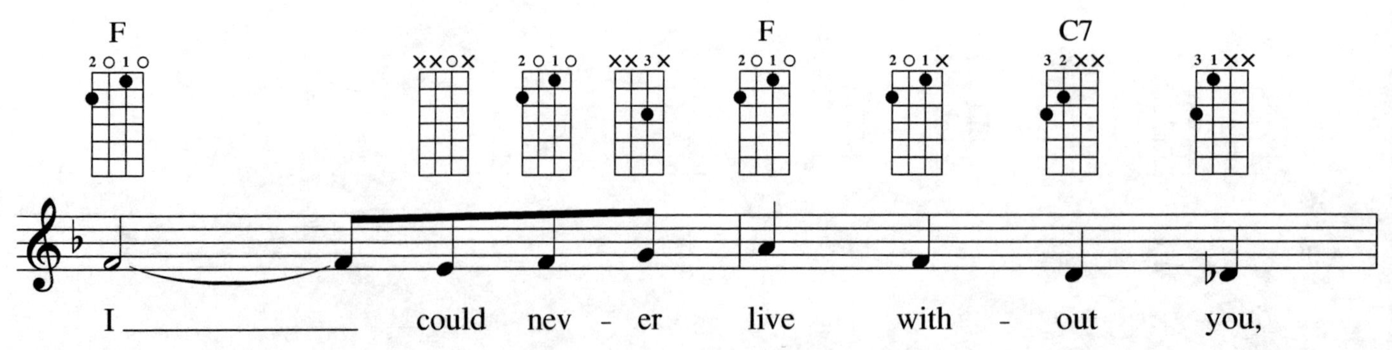
F
F
C7
I could nev - er live with - out you,

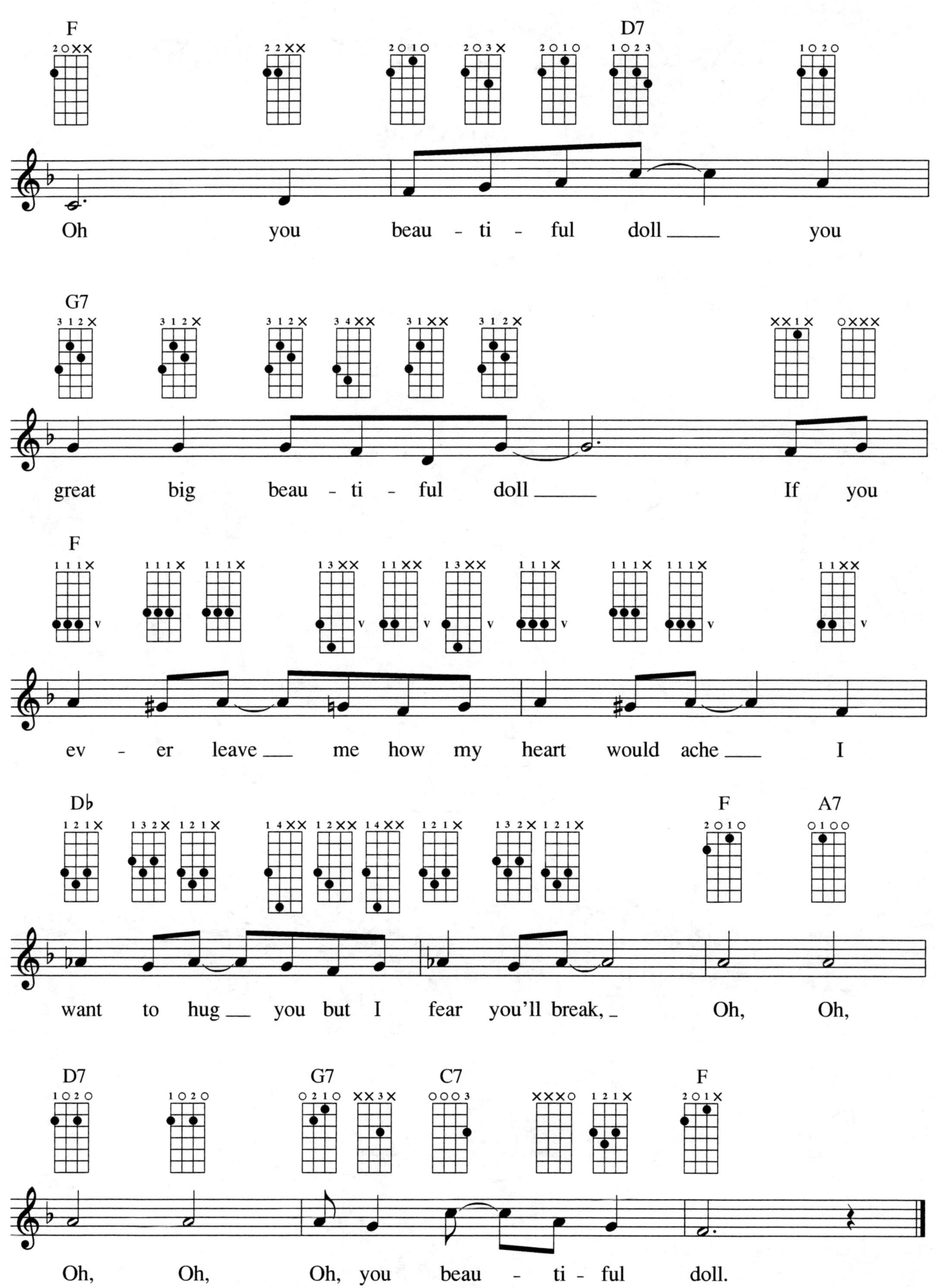
F D7
Oh you beau - ti - ful doll you
G7
great big beau - ti - ful doll If you
F
ev - er leave me how my heart would ache I
D♭ F A7
want to hug you but I fear you'll break, Oh, Oh,
D7 G7 C7 F
Oh, Oh, Oh, you beau - ti - ful doll.

Basic Uke Chord Chart

MAJOR Chords

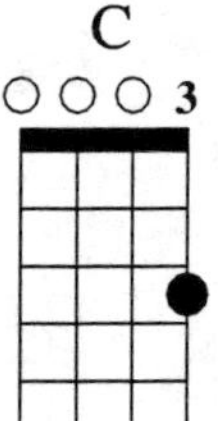
C
○ ○ ○ 3

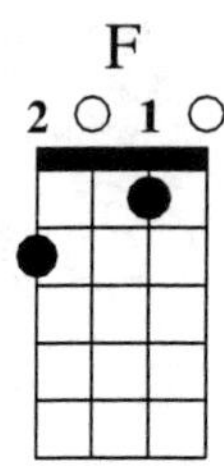
F
2 ○ 1 ○

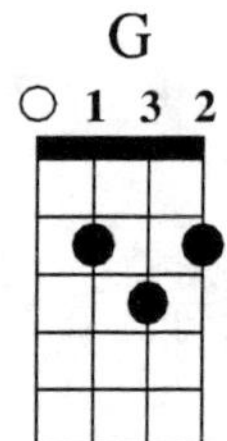
G
○ 1 3 2

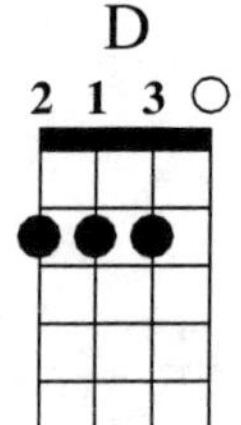
D
2 1 3 ○

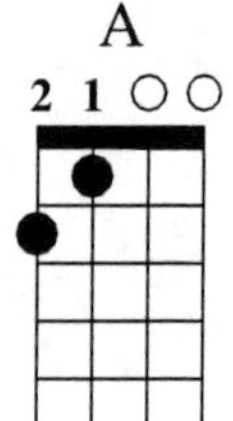
A
2 1 ○ ○

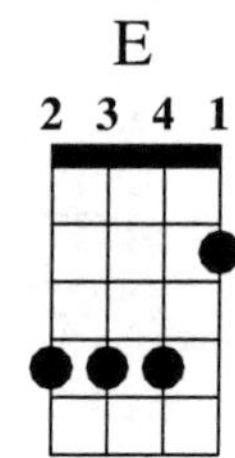
E
2 3 4 1

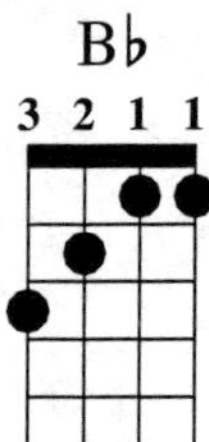
B♭
3 2 1 1

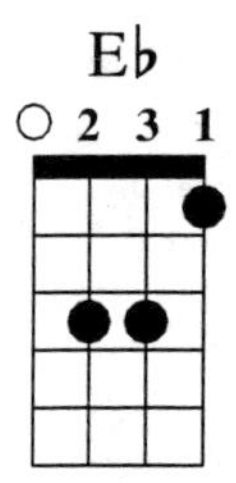
E♭
○ 2 3 1

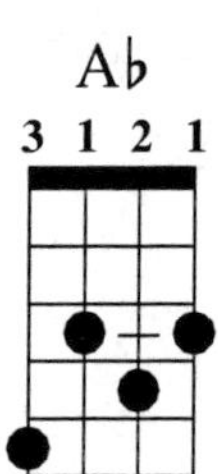
A♭
3 1 2 1

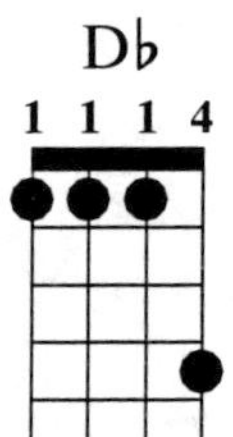
D♭
1 1 1 4

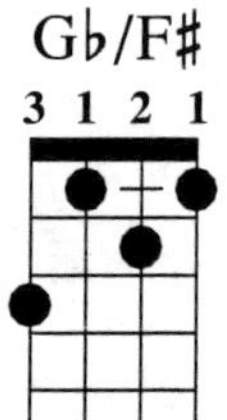
G♭/F♯
3 1 2 1

B
3 2 1 1

MINOR Chords

Cm
○ 1 1 1

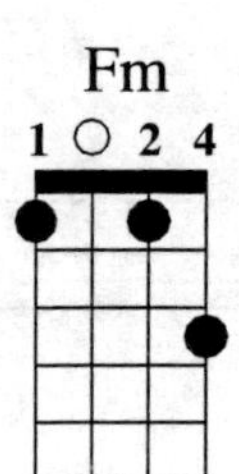
Fm
1 ○ 2 4

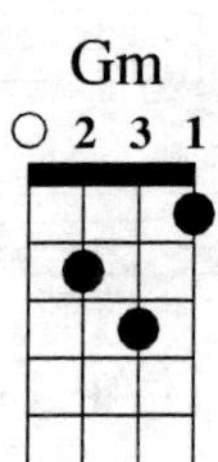
Gm
○ 2 3 1

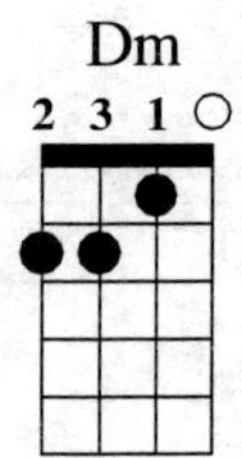
Dm
2 3 1 ○

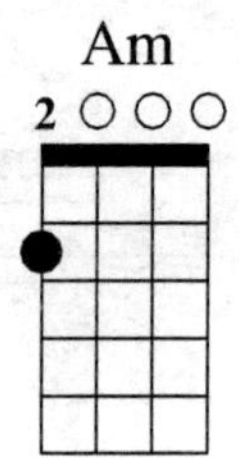
Am
2 ○ ○ ○

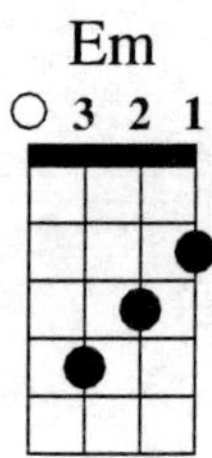
Em
○ 3 2 1

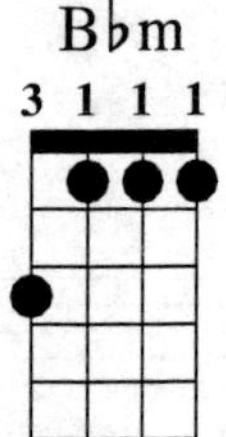
B♭m
3 1 1 1

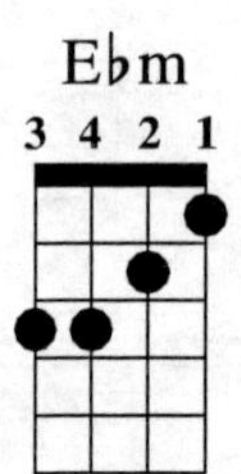
E♭m
3 4 2 1

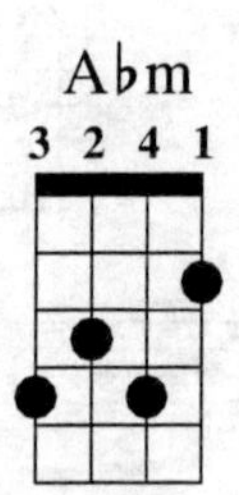
A♭m
3 2 4 1

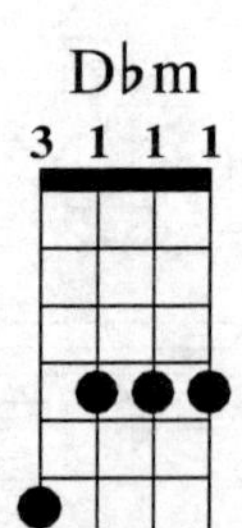
D♭m
3 1 1 1

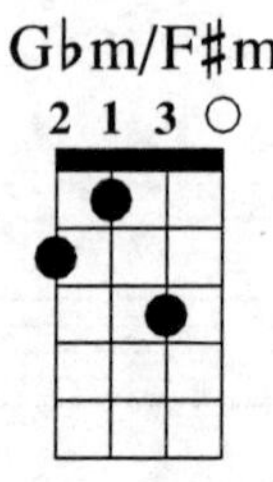
G♭m/F♯m
2 1 3 ○

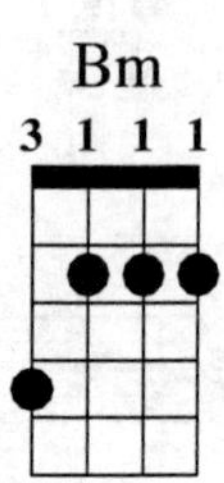
Bm
3 1 1 1

SEVENTH Chords

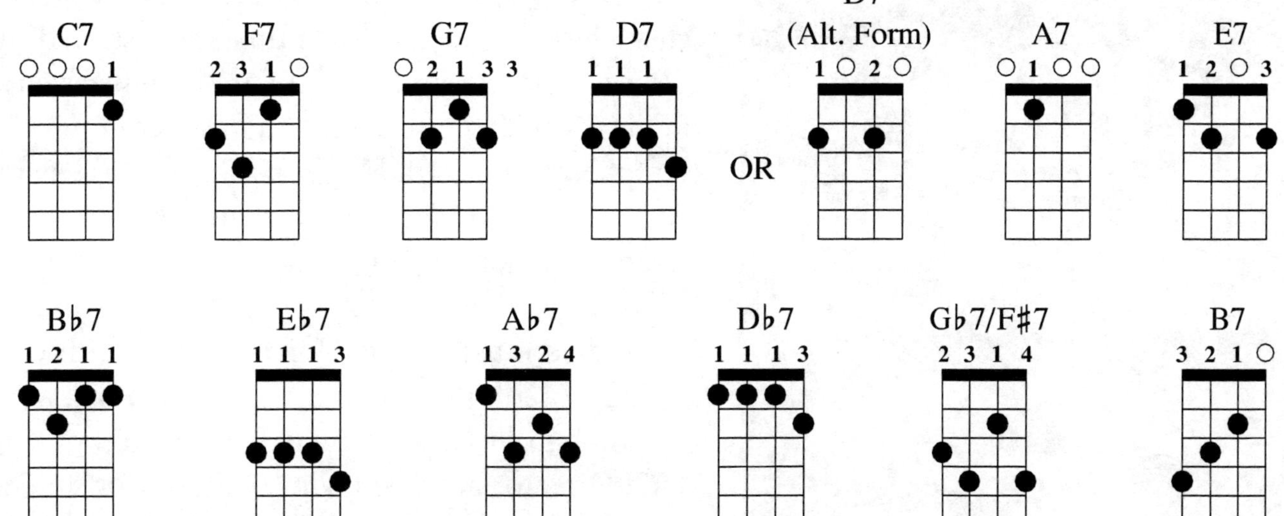

C7
F7
G7
D7
OR
D7 (Alt. Form)
A7
E7
B♭7
E♭7
A♭7
D♭7
G♭7/F♯7
B7

DIMINISHED Chords

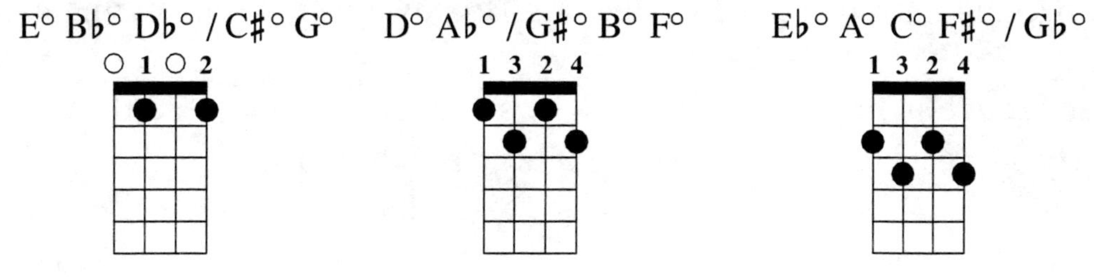

E° B♭° D♭° / C♯° G°
D° A♭° / G♯° B° F°
E♭° A° C° F♯° / G♭°

AUGMENTED Chords

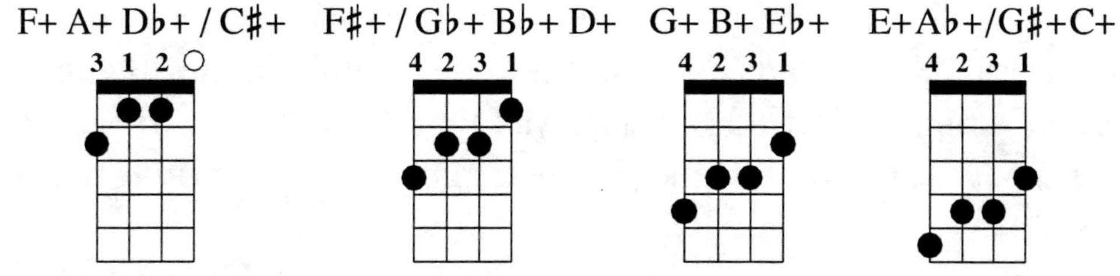

F+ A+ D♭+ / C♯+
F♯+ / G♭+ B♭+ D+
G+ B+ E♭+
E+A♭+/G♯+C+

For complete Photo/Diagram Chord Listing see

Mel Bay's *Ukulele Chord Book* (MB93269)

NEIL GRIFFIN

Neil Griffin was born in Charlotte, North Carolina. Music has always been his prime interest, starting wtih clarinet instruction in the fifth grade and learning guitar on his own. He performed as a member of the Charlotte Symphony Orchestra at age 15 playing bass clarinet. He also began performing with area dance bands on saxophone, clarinet, and guitar.

He studied music at the Univeristy of North Carolina at Chapel Hill, playing First Chair Alto Sax as a freshman in the UNC Concert Band. Neil taught as Band Director at three county schools for several years and at the same time privately for Kidd-Frix Music Co. in their Charlotte accordion school. When the school was purchased by Music Inc. Neil went into management and retail music sales for them. At the same time, Neil played regularly with his own band for wedding receptions, office parties, etc., and gained valuable experience from playing summer theater for many well-known stars as well as being called on a regular basis to play banjo, guitar, and clarinet for traveling Broadway shows appearing in the area.

Neil was very active in the Charlotte Musicians Association and served as president for approximately 13 years as well as holding other executive offices.

Some of the first professional jobs Neil played were good old southern square dances, which at that time weren't as fancy as they are today but provided him with an appreciation for country and bluegrass music that was never forgotten. He enjoyed doing 5 radio shows and two TV shows per week at WBT and WBTV in Charlotte for over a year.

In the early 60's Neil was hired to manage Tillman Music Co. in Charlotte. There he helped in starting the Aria Pro II line of instruments. Neil and his brother Steve, who also writes for Mel Bay Publications, went into the music-school business together in the 70's and later expanded as a retail music store. During this period Neil met Mel Bay and began to write material for 5-string banjo which was pretty scarce at the time. He thoroughly enjoyed writing and teaching.

He has authored or co-authored several books for Mel Bay Publications on the subjects of 5-string banjo, rock guitar, and accordion.